MW00906670

Mister Fishback's

# Monster

*Steve Sabatka*

BLACK BED
SHEET

Mister Fishback's Monster
A Black Bed Sheet/Diverse Media E-Book
August 2016

Library of Congress Control Number: 2016951765

ISBN 10: 0-99792761-5
ISBN 13: 978-0-9979276-1-0

# Mister Fishback's Monster

**A Black Bed Sheet/Diverse Media Book**
Antelope, CA

# Mister Fishback's Monster

## Steve Sabatka

# Prologue

People always ask me about the photo I keep here at the TV studio where I work: Three young friends with laughing smiles – and filthy, blood-spattered faces. I'm the kid in the middle, the one holding the bug-eyed ferret with Frankenstein scars around the top of his head.

That picture is actually a frame of eight millimeter film, blown up to an eight-by-ten photograph, taken during the most eventful week of our lives. Spring Break of my sophomore year, 1978.

A lot happened during that Sensoramic, E-ticket, thrill-ride-of-a-week. It started off with me getting a black eye. Then a terrifying sea monster came ashore to wreak havoc in our little coastal town. Really. The most powerful man in the state sent one of his hired goons to choke me. I finally, finally went toe-to-toe with the greatest tragedy of my life. And I actually figured out Herman Melville's classic novel, *Moby Dick*. Well, maybe.

Last but not least, I made passionate, nose-on-nose love with Pam Grier. More than once, I might add. You damn straight.

I can't help but smile and laugh and get a little teary-eyed every time I tell people the story behind that picture. When I tell it, I can almost see it in my mind, like scenes from the kind of movie you'd watch late on a Saturday night. And the special effects are great.

# -Part One-

"Whenever I find myself growing grim about the mouth; whenever it is a damp, drizzly November in my soul; whenever I find myself involuntarily pausing before coffin warehouses, and bringing up the rear of every funeral I meet; and especially whenever my hypos get such an upper hand of me, that it requires a strong moral **principle** to prevent me from deliberately stepping into the street, and methodically knocking people's hats off - then, I account it high time to get to sea as soon as I can."
— *Moby Dick*, Herman Melville, 1851

"Movies for me are a heightened reality. Making reality fun to live with, as opposed to something you run from and protect yourself from."
— Steven Spielberg, 1978

"Imaginary lovers
Never let you down."
— "Imaginary Lover," The Atlanta Rhythm Section, 1978

"You're welcome to visit Oregon, but please don't stay."
— Oregon Governor Tom McCall, 1973

# Chapter One

The chipmunks came out first. To this day, I don't know if chipmunks travel in herds or schools or packs or what, but at least three hundred of the little brown critters, all caught up in some kind of buck tooth freak out, came flooding out of the forest, across the mossy ground, and then off to the south.

Odd, I thought.

Next, a dozen or so deer. Spotted, spindle-leg fawns first, then does, and then Bambi-dad bucks, came bounding, pogo sticking, after the chipmunks, and their round brown eyes were wide with terror.

Were the woods on fire?

Then elk, fifteen, twenty, maybe, as majestic as any animal on Earth – and obviously aware of that fact – cleared the Douglas fir trees and the Scotch broom, their muscles rippling, their nostrils wet and flared and blasting white steam. They scattered, regrouped, and then followed the chipmunks and the deer to safety.

And then I saw what had caused all those animals to flee in mad fear.

Teeth. Six-inch, ivory-colored, meat-tearing teeth, set in a jaw that jutted out like the bucket of a steam shovel, low to the ground at first, then rising, ten, twenty, twenty-five feet into the air. Reptile eyes, iridescent and searching for prey. Tiny, two-clawed forearms, twitching with anticipation.

*"It came without warning, a ravenous refugee from the*

*dawn of time, reawakened to terrorize an unsuspecting world!"*

A Tyrannosaurus Rex – not just any T. Rex, and certainly not the kind of Rex you might remember from little kids' dinosaur books or cartoons, but the Alpha Rex, the Ultra Rex, the Rex's Rex, the very Jack Palance of Tyrant Lizards, black as a water moccasin, steaming in the chill, second period air, and seemingly grinning at the punch line of the meanest, scariest joke ever told – shouldered its way out of the tree line and onto the football field of Oswald West High School.

I was the only one in Ms. Ellerath's language arts class who saw the beast, and the only one who heard the corny voice.

*"Watch, as a prehistoric monster emerges from a bygone age to terrify modern humanity!"*

Julie Smith, blond and beautiful in a quiet, fragile, almost angelic sort of way, was reading the assigned book – *Moby Dick*. Her scoliosis brace wouldn't let her easily turn to one side or the other, so she didn't see the dinosaur.

My friend, Mihn, reading the same book, and actually understanding it, wouldn't have noticed a dozen prehistoric carnivores until one of them actually snatched him up by the hood of the red sweatshirt he wore every day, flipped him up in the air, and then caught him on the way back down like a dog biscuit.

Ronny Behr, a big kid with a scraggily beard that looked like rusty steel wool, was doodling in his notebook, not reading, not caring – and completely oblivious to the Tyrannosaurus. When Ronny caught me looking at him, he mouthed the words "shit-head freak," and gave me the finger. Thing is, he didn't have any "bird" finger. Just a stump. Oh, great. That was his way of reminding me that he was still pissed off about The Cyclops Incident.

2

More about that later.

Ms. Ellerath sat at her desk with her back to both the window and the approaching horror. She had been reading to the class from Herman Melville's classic, and trying to explain to us that the *Pequod*, Captain Ahab's whaling ship, painted black and decorated with whale bones and skulls and teeth, was actually a literary symbol for death. Ms. Ellerath liked that kind of thing. Symbolism. Metaphor. Deeper meaning.

But we just didn't get it, or even care. The book our teacher loved so much had left us open-mouth bored. And so, after several attempts to engage us, Ms. Ellerath had quit in frustration – and gave us all a homework assignment.

"When you come back from your break," she said, "I want a two-page essay that answers the following classic, timeless question about this novel: Why is Moby Dick white? Why did Melville make this choice? What is the symbolism involved?"

White? Symbolism? I had no earthly idea why Moby Dick was white. Judging by the grumbles and gripes I heard just then, neither did anyone else in the class. And who assigns homework over Spring Break?

And that's when I first saw the beast – which wasn't a murderous, monochromatic whale with a bent jaw and a hide all stuck with twisted harpoons and rusty lances, but a slavering refugee from the Cretaceous period – mad with hunger, and sniffing the wooden bleachers, now, perhaps lured by the residual smell of human butts from the last track meet.

Call me Steve. It wasn't unusual for me to imagine prehistoric beasts, mythical monsters, radioactive mutations, and all kinds of nightmare creatures, in what I called Steve-O-Scope: a widescreen, Technicolor, intense kind of daydream, complete with quadrophonic sound. And it wasn't unusual for me to hear an authoritative and vaguely familiar voice, straight out of a B-movie trailer.

Movie Trailer Guy: *"See antediluvian terror, unleashed on an unsuspecting world!"*

I didn't actually see things that didn't exist, and I didn't hear voices, but several times a day, I escaped into my own fantasy land. Out of boredom, sometimes. But mostly out of fear. Monsters roared and stomped through my imaginary world, but nobody really got hurt or killed there. And drunk drivers never murdered people you loved.

Dinosaurs and monsters were more than just a fantasy for me, though, because unlike most tenth grade boys, my heroes weren't rock stars or athletes. My role models were men like Willis O'Brien, the man that gave King Kong frame-by-frame, chest-beating life, and Ray Harryhausen, who animated the screaming army of skeletons in *Jason and the Argonauts*.

Most guys in my class wanted to be loggers or fishermen. But I wanted to make monsters, bring dinosaurs back from extinction. As a career. Nerdy? Geekish? Maybe. But I'd rather be locked away in a tiny studio with a movie camera and my little rubber monsters than lose an arm or a leg in a logging accident and slowly bleed out into a pile of sawdust, or be knocked off the transom of a shrimp trawler by a rogue wave and then either freeze to death and drown.

Just outside the classroom window, the Rex peered in at us. Ms. Ellerath, not two feet away from those ancient eyes, that mass of cruel teeth, and protected only by thin glass, mumbled to herself about apathetic students. When the T. Rex reached out with one of those palsied forearms, its claws squeaked

4

against the window, and that sound made me cringe.

I made my own amateur flicks. (I never had the guts to call them movies or films.) And I spent long hours in my dad's auto repair shop behind our house, animating creatures I had sculpted out of plasticine and clicking off single frames with my Keystone Model K8, regular eight millimeter movie camera. Regular eight. It was an old war horse, but it got the job done.

The Rex scratched again, again, like a dog wanting inside.

My flicks, *Reptilla*, Son of *Reptilla*, *Lewis and Clark Find a Dinosaur* (which was based on a true story, by the way) weren't what you'd call Hollywood quality. But considering the equipment I had to work with, and budgets that depended on how many strawberries and green beans I picked in the summer and how many lawns I mowed in the spring, they weren't half bad. My handmade monsters moved a little jerkily. My human actors – friends, mostly – were only slightly more believable.

But I was learning, and getting better. I hoped that my current project, *Epoch Lost*, would be different – more creative, more professional – than my other flicks. And I hoped it would be good enough to get me into film school after I graduated.

The Tyrannosaurus pressed the side of its head against the window, watching Ms. Ellerath with slitted pupils and smearing the glass with rabid froth. I studied the animal's mist-slick, coal-colored skin. The layers of muscle, bunching and relaxing over strong bones and joints. Those pathetic forelimbs, like plucked chicken wings. Dark, prehistoric blood, pulsing through veins and arteries. I could never achieve the same kind of realism with dime store clay and Kodachrome film.

The starving, frustrated beast was about to crash through that window and then snap up Ms. Ellerath, dog-eared, underlined copy of *Moby Dick*, and all.

*"Can your heart stand the suspense?"*

So it was a good thing that Pam Grier appeared when she did. That's right, Pam Grier, the Afro-wearin' star of *Foxy Brown*, *Coffy* and several other R-rated action movies made in the seventies. I was in love with her.

*"She's sweet brown sugar with a touch of spice. And a whole mess of trouble if you don't treat her nice!"*

Why was a white kid on the Oregon Coast, the son of an auto mechanic and a roller derby queen, in love with Pam Grier and not Farah Fawcett Majors or Cheryl Tiegs? Well, it wasn't just Pam's body — spectacular as it was.

*"That sistah is stacked, and that's a fact!"*

It was her nose. No joke. My Pam had the proud, noble nose of a warrior queen, and that nose drove me hormone-rush crazy. I don't know why.

Of course, Pam Grier had karate-chopped and drop-kicked and bar-stooled a hundred crooked cops and dope-pushers and pimps. Maybe a thousand. But to the best of my knowledge, she had never gone up against an Ultra Rex. Hands on hips, now, and wearing nursing scrubs for some reason, Pam didn't seem at all concerned. She scolded the Rex, which bared its teeth and snarled and was about to snatch her up in those two-fingered claws and bite her 'fro-sportin' head right off, until admonished a second time: "Don't make me whup up on you, jive turkey!"

Humbled, cowed, the T. Rex lowered its head, allowing Pam — nostrils flaring — to climb up to the top of its back where there was a saddle, crafted of leather and mahogany. Pam sat down, and when she scratched the top of the dinosaur's head with strong but impeccably manicured fingers, the Rex closed its eyes because that was its favorite spot, and one of his legs thumped on the ground like a happy dog.

"Now, that's better!"

My baby kicked her bare heels behind the Rex's lower jaw, and the great carnivore stood and turned back to the trees. Then Pam waved to me from over her shoulder, blew me a hot kiss, and rode the Tyrannosaurus back into the forest.

Back to reality. Ms. Ellerath loved books as much as I loved movies, but she couldn't get her students to care. Maybe things would've been different if she'd had better special effects. Either way, she didn't deserve to get chomped by a T. Rex.

The bell rang. "Have a good break," Ms. Ellerath said, without smiling

Sudden homework assignment aside, I was jazzed. After all, I was on the teeter edge of a week-long break. No school. Getting some work done on my flick. Good times with my friends. It sure sounded great. Of course, I didn't know it at the time, but I was about to take a pounding – and a monster more terrifying than anything that ever stomped or slithered out of Hollywood was headed for Seaport.

*"And this time, it would not be imaginary!"*

# Chapter Two

The Beach Boys never sang about the Oregon Coast, and Annette Funicello and Frankie Avalon never made a beach movie here. Why? For one thing, it rains a lot on the coast – seventy inches or more each year – and sometimes that rain blows in off the sea at sixty-five miles an hour, which is enough to knock a big man on his butt. The ocean itself is too cold for swimming, although there never seems to be a shortage of insane surfers out in the chop, despite the occasional orca sighting. But we coasters enjoy the pure, clean rain and we like to watch as waves roll in from the far horizon and crash against rocky cliffs, and we love to walk on the beach after a storm, not seeing another living soul, or even any other footprints in the sand, knowing that this is the way it was before Lewis and Clark showed up and a million years before that.

To me, the Oregon Coast is a *haiku* kind of place.

*The sea, gray and green.*
*The rain falls clear from the sky.*
*When does the rain change?*

Seaport was a typical, almost postcard coastal town: Hotels with big anchors out on the front lawns. Chainsaw woodcarvings of whales and sea captains and Vikings. Streaks and glops of white and black seagull poop. Restaurants, promising THE BEST CLAM CHOWDER ON THE OREGON COAST.

Salt-rusted pickup trucks, their beds stacked with crab rings and fishing gear. You could see the Pacific Ocean from almost anywhere in town – if you looked to the west, that is. At night you could hear the low rumble of waves and the barking of sea lions, and the fog horn, booming out from the Cape Cook lighthouse.

At the time, most Seaporters were from middle-class and lower-class, hard-working families. Like I said, Dad was a motor-head, but most fathers worked on fishing boats or somewhere up on the summit, cutting trees. Some were construction workers. Ma didn't work outside our home, but most moms worked in that part of Seaport we all called The Pier – the fishing part of town – shuckin' oysters, shakin' crabs, packin' boxes, and not smellin' very motherly when they came home from work.

Back then, nearly everyone in Seaport was Caucasian. White, that is, like Moby Dick, and I guess there is a metaphor in there somewhere. There were lots of fifth and sixth-generation Finns and Norskies, like Ma. Dad came from a long line of Euro-mutts but called himself a Californian.

But if you took the time, you could see Hispanic men, stocking the boats with ice early in the morning and then unloading the tuna and halibut and shrimp at the end of the day. There were two or three Asian families in town, Mihn's being among them. And there was Pam Grier, of course, kicking ass on the rain slick screen of the Beacon Drive In Theater. And in my head.

At one time, a hundred years before I was born, and long before that, everyone that lived along the Oregon Coast belonged to one of the old coastal tribes: Siuslaw, Chinook, Salishan. But those original folks were all gone, now, as far as I could tell. Run off. Whittled down. All that was left of the old tribes were the Indian names on hotels and street signs, yellowed photographs in the county museum – and maybe one, half-crazy old timer. More about him later.

People in Seaport had their place, their own unique niche in the order of things, and so did every kid in the Oz cafeteria. The jocks. Nerds. Cheerleaders. Skankdogs. The special kids. Ronny Behr and his fellow low-boaters. Other assorted types and sub-types.

And there were the three of us, sitting close to the teachers' table because it was a little safer there, and as far away as we could get from the back of the cafeteria, the place we called the DMZ. Bad stuff happened there. Fights. Beatings. Random acts of meandom.

*"It was a haven and breeding ground for all manner of juvenile cruelty!"*

I was a tenth-grade dinosaur tamer, a skinny, tall and getting taller every day kid, with a home-done haircut, clothes that I outgrew every few months – and weirdo eyeglasses, Frankensteined together out of my grandfather's antique wire rim frames, other parts I'd found at garage sales, and my own prescription lenses. I wanted to look like a mad scientist, but looking back, I probably looked more like one of those Japanese soldiers that didn't know the war had ended. Only taller. "Why is Moby Dick white?"

Mihn sat across from me. "In my culture, the color white is a symbol of death." The Vietnam War had ended a few years before, and Mihn's family had escaped from that country, making their way across the South China Sea, just after the capitol, Saigon, was overrun by the bad guys. Mihn was a small, shy kid

10

with black hair, curious brown eyes behind Clark Kent glasses, a pretty cool accent, and, like I said before, a red sweatshirt. He was also a genuinely nice person. His dad had a charter fishing business in town. "Herman Melville was not Vietnamese, though."

"White can also stand for purity, innocence." Kenneth J. Hull was a senior, a wrestler, a hard rocker in the age of disco, and he always sat with Mihn. At 250 plus pounds, Ken was in what his coaches called "the unlimited" class. He wore a crew cut, a perpetual three-day beard, pants that were always a bit too short, exposing white socks above his tennis shoes – and a letterman jacket. But Ken wasn't one of the jocks. He didn't fit in with that bunch. Maybe it was because he had moved to Seaport from Alaska, and lived with his grandmother because his "Pops" was gone fishing a lot. Maybe it was because he was on the chess team. And maybe it was because he had a beautiful tenor voice. Ken was committed to his own moral code, a loyal friend, and there wasn't an ounce of bully in him. Ken also had a car: a way-cool, bone-white, two-door, 1963 Thunderbird with a slightly crunched rear bumper.

"Maybe Moby Dick was just very clean," I said.

Julie Smith always sat at our table, too, but away from the three of us, and always eating alone. Have you ever noticed how girls pick their sandwiches apart with their fingers? Julie did that, too. I thought Julie was pretty, despite that metal neck brace – and her relatively small nose.

I always brought my own lunch, usually just a peanut butter and cheese sandwich, milk, and some carrot or celery sticks in a plastic baggie. Ma was a great cook. She had grown up cooking for the crew on her dad's crab boat, so even her peanut butter sandwiches – chunky peanut butter on sourdough bread with an extra thin slice of cheddar – were a cut above. (Her tuna casserole was terrible, but she only made that when she was mad at Dad.)

Sometimes, Ma packed a cupcake in my lunch, and whenever she did, I always gave it to Julie. I don't know why. It wasn't because I felt sorry for her, because I knew that anyone who had to deal with scoliosis and that metal brace must be a strong person and certainly didn't need any of my sympathy. Julie just seemed like a good person who was dealing with a bad break. She always thanked me, but we never talked, and that was OK.

"What is the name of this dish?" Mihn loved cafeteria food. Loved it. To him, Turkey Tetrazzini, fish sticks, and beef and noodles were some sort of exotic cuisine. He was especially fond of tater tots of all things. Tater tots. Can you believe it?

And today, Mihn was in for a treat. There was something new on the menu.

"Chili mac." I wondered if Mihn and his family used chopsticks when they ate. I had been at Mihn's house only one time. His mom had been very nice to me.

"Ahh . . ." Mihn leaned over his plastic lunch tray and his glasses steamed up. "It smells spicy."

"Southwestern classic." Ken had already finished his own chili mac. The back of his hand was smeared with tomato sauce as he pointed his fork at the other compartments on Mihn's tray. "Your basic frozen corn nibblets. Reconstituted mashed potatoes, created by NASA. Canned applesauce."

"Nibblets?" Mihn rubbed his hands together

"Nibblets." Ken took a six-inch pepperoni stick from inside his letterman jacket, and sniffed it as if it was a fine cigar. He bit off the tip, spat it out, and stuck the pepperoni in his mouth.

Mihn was about to savor his first ever mouthful of chili mac . . .

. . . when Ken nudged him. "It's Mai!"

Mihn dropped his fork.

Mai was pretty – beautiful – with a quiet face and long, long black hair. She had played Sacajawea in *Lewis and Clark Find a Dinosaur*, but all she really did was just stand there while Ken and Mihn, playing the famous explorers, did all the over-acting. Ken had been in love with her ever since.

"Thank you, Ken." Mihn glared behind foggy lenses. "I would not have recognized my own sister without your help."

Mai smiled at me, completely ignored Ken, and sat down on Mihn's other side.

One of the many advantages of having an imaginary girlfriend: She can't ignore you.

As Mihn and Mai conversed in a foreign, sing-songy language, Ken stared at Mai and switched his pepperoni stick back and forth from one side of his mouth to the other. Then Mai left.

"What did she want?" Ken asked. "What did she say?"

Mihn was a reserved, quiet guy most of the time, but every once in a while, he threw a rod. "None of your business, stupid ass stick, anyway!" Mihn's English was good, but his cussing seemed to consist entirely of the word "ass."

"Give me a break," Ken said. "I'm almost family!"

"Family?" Mihn was confused.

"Think about it." Ken wrapped his arm around Mihn. "When I marry Mai, I'll be your brother-in-law!"

"That will never ass happen!"

Ken and Mihn argued sometimes, but they were good friends. We were all good friends.

"Interesting thing about your Asiatic female." Ken sat back and burped chili mac. "She's quiet, seemingly docile, yet possessed of a certain quiet, inner strength."

Mihn's glasses had cleared by now. "My mother is an Asiatic female, you know."

Ken rubbed his stubble, and considered this point.

Mihn winced. "Who knows what kind of disgusting thoughts go through your head when you cast your beady eyes on my innocent sister!"

Ken took offense. "You underestimate me," he said. "My intentions are entirely honorable." I'm sure he meant that.

"Ass train." Mihn picked up his fork. But he didn't get a chance to taste chili mac. Something, I didn't know what just then, hit me square in the right eye. My glasses cut into the bridge of my nose.

There was an explosion of noise. Shouts and screams. Laughter.

My eye stung and watered up when I tried to open it, so I just kept it shut. I felt blood on my nose.

"Are you OK?" Mihn asked. "What an ass thing to do to somebody!"

"Yep." With my one good eye, I saw my specs lying twisted on the table. And I saw an orange, as big as a softball, flattened on one side and resting now, in Mihn's chili mac.

"And for desert, an orange, no doubt harvested from the lush Hood River Valley." Ken stood, pepperoni stick clenched between gritted teeth, and quickly surveyed the cafeteria. His eyes locked in on some especially incriminating detail or another. Then he yelled, *"Sic semper tyrannis!"* and bounded off into the DMZ.

For a big guy, Ken moved fast. Everybody got out of his way.

I didn't follow Ken. But my Ultra Rex suddenly returned out of nowhere – without Pam Grier on his back – and stomped off into the DMZ with its head down, upending tables and tossing meal trays and students as it went.

*"The beast was crazed with a primitive craving for blood soaked revenge!"*

Mass panic ensued. Cheerleaders screamed. Teachers ran for cover. When the Rex reached the dark heart of the DMZ, it searched for anyone that had ever been cruel to anyone smaller, weaker, or less than physically perfect. And when the Rex found those poor devils, it caught them in that horrific mouth and chomped down and shook its head back and forth like a dog with a rope toy. Heads and limbs fell, bloody and twitching, to the ground. It was an awful thing to see and hear.

*"To avoid fainting, keep repeating, it's only a movie. It's only a movie!"*

A loud thud stopped the Ultra Rex. It was the sound of a big fist punching a furry, bully face. Groans. Then another thud. Teachers got up from their table, and a few jogged off and into the DMZ. My Tyrannosaurus vanished.

Ms. Ellerath sat down next to me and put her arm around me.

"I'm sorry," she said. "There's a cut on your nose. Let's go see the nurse."

"You should see the nurse," Mihn said.

"OK." When I got up from the table, people laughed.

15

"Finish your lunch!" Ms. Ellerath yelled – or tried to – but her voice kind of cracked at the end of the sentence. She wasn't much of a yeller, I guess.

"Make a hole and make it wide!" Our **principal**, Mister Schafer, a Korean War vet with a flat top cut and leather-lookin' creases on the back of his neck, was a good yeller. He came striding out of the DMZ, holding two boys by their collars. "I'll suspend you two back to the Stone Age!"

One of the boys was, surprise, surprise, Ronny Behr, laughing and covering his nose with one hand. Blood dripped from between his fingers and onto the cafeteria floor. The other boy was Ken, wringing the knuckles of his right hand and biting on that last tiny stub of pepperoni and looking a little lost. I nodded my head in his direction as a sign of appreciation, but I don't think he noticed.

As Ronny passed, he stuck what was left of his bird finger at me.

"What does that mean?" Ms. Ellerath asked.

"It must be some kind of bully sign language." I didn't feel like explaining The Cyclops Incident at the moment.

On the way out of the cafeteria, I looked at Julie. She was looking at me. There were tears in her eyes.

# Chapter Three

I sat in the school nurse's office. My camera eye hurt. So did my nose. The ice pack helped a little.

This was my first time in Nurse Nugent's office, and I was a titch disappointed that it didn't look at all like Doctor Frankenstein's laboratory. No bubbling flasks or test tubes or big metal rigs to draw lightning down out of the sky to reanimate a stitched-together corpse. Not a single skull.

Down the hall, Ronny Behr was sitting on the bench outside Mister Schafer's office, waiting for someone to come pick him up. He had been suspended for two days. Ken had been suspended for the rest of the day and had already gone home.

I felt bad for Ken. He had stood up for me. He had gotten himself suspended from school because of me. I should've been the one to go stomping off into the DMZ to thrash Ronny Behr.

"I think we should send Steve home." Nurse Nugent was on the phone, telling Ma what had happened at lunch. Orange to the face. Black eye. Bully suspended. All that jazz. She smiled and winked at me. "It's Friday, after all, and Spring Break starts tomorrow." Sounded good to me. I needed a break.

I could hear Ma on the other end of the line. She thanked the nurse, told her not to send me home – and to make sure I got to my next class on time.

Thanks, Ma.

"I'll be sure and do just that." Nurse Nugent knew better than to argue with Ma. Everybody knew better.

The bell rang. Lunch was over. Time for fifth period. Nurse Nugent hung up the phone then she looked at me with a sad expression on her face. "Sorry, Steve," she said. "Your mom wants you to stay. How's your eye doing?"

"It's OK." I handed her the ice pack.

"Do you know why Ronny Behr threw that orange at you?"

"Beats me." It was because of The Cyclops.

Mister Schafer stood in the doorway. "Is this boy ready for duty?"

"Ready as he'll ever be," Nurse Nugent said.

"Let's go," Mister Schafer said. "I'll escort you to class. Who is your fifth period teacher?"

"Mister Fishback," I said. "Marine biology."

"See you later, Steve." Nurse Nugent looked like she felt bad for me.

"Thanks." I followed Mister Schafer down the hall to Mister Fishback's room, and took my usual seat next to Mihn, my lab partner. Everyone else in the room was quiet. I mean silent. It was obvious that Mister Fishback, standing there at the front of the room with his arms folded across his chest, had warned them not to laugh or say anything or give me any grief.

I was grateful for that. Very grateful. Still am. Mister Fishback was my favorite teacher. He loved his subject, and he made it interesting. If I hadn't had my heart set on being a special effects artist, I might have considered a career as a marine biologist. Or maybe a marine paleontologist.

I don't know if anyone was staring at me because I didn't even look up – except once, and for just a second, to see the expression on Julie Smith's face. And I was surprised. She looked like she had been

18

waiting for me, and that she was glad that I was OK.

"Shall we begin?" Mister Fishback seemed to have stepped out of some mysterious seafaring past, and would've been right at home in *Moby Dick*. Tall, thin, he had a dark beard with no mustache, just like those little woodcarvings of sea captains you see in curio shops, and on the window sill above the sink in Ma's avocado colored kitchen. Sometimes, Mister F. wore a stuffed, flea-bitten parrot on his shoulder so that he looked like some goofy, garage sale pirate.

But not today. When someone at the back of the room tried to suppress a snicker and didn't do a very good job of it, Mister Fishback leaned forward, ready to pounce on somebody and chew some butt. "Excuse me?"

Silence once again.

Sometimes, Mister F. spoke with an East Coast accent. "That's *bettah.*"

Mister Fishback's classroom was like a museum, or maybe Captain Nemo's private study, a place where he could go to relax after a hard day of blowing up war ships: There were old maps and nautical charts on the walls. Books with brittle pages that smelled of sulfur. Antique microscopes. Racks of test tubes and twisted flasks. A harpoon, its iron lance inscribed with Japanese characters and gleaming with a thin sheen of oil.

And specimen jars. Those antique, hand blown glass jars, sealed with wide corks and gathered in neat rows on a shelf up above Mister Fishback's desk, contained marine specimens, all hovering in murky formaldehyde. Those dead specimens all looked like they might blink at any moment, jump at you just for the fun of it, and then chuckle at your reaction like so many evil, pickled Muppets.

19

Each of those puckered and pruny creatures was identified by a paper label with a neatly typed, Latin name.

Sepia elegans
Stiliger bellulus
Eledone cirrhosa
Anemonactis mazeli

I thought those specimen jars would look cool in Nurse Nugent's office.

In his off time, Mister Fishback was a surfer and a runner, and had been friends with Steve Prefontaine before the track star's tragic death. Mister F. preferred the beach to any track, though, but hadn't been running much lately – ever since dropping an antique diving helmet on his foot during a lesson about deep-sea diving. I'd never heard a teacher use that kind of language.

The subject of today's lesson: *Architeuthis*, the giant squid. "We know almost nothing about these fascinating animals. How long do they live? How large can they grow?" As Mister Fishback limped back and forth in front of the classroom, I imagined that his right leg had been replaced by a shaft of lathed ivory. "Nobody has ever seen a giant squid alive in its natural habitat. Dead remains have washed ashore, and we've seen sucker scars on dead sperm whales, each a foot in diameter, etched deep into the whales' skin. Just imagine a fight between a monster whale and a giant squid."

I wondered then and I wonder now if Mister Fishback wasn't trying to throw me some kind of fantasy bone, give me a mental image so that I could tune out and relax after getting smacked in the kisser with an orange. I sure needed an excuse to go away for a while. Of course, that would mean that he somehow knew about my Steve-O-Scope spectaculars, and that doesn't seem likely. Does it? Did he need to escape, too, sometimes?

I didn't latch on to that squid vs. whale scene, though, because I just happened to be staring at those glass jars. They were shaking, vibrating in time with the teacher's words. And the things inside those jars were flexing and throbbing and pushing against the glass, all at the same time, with a common rhythm. A pulse. Dead eyes rolled and blinked and searched for a way out.

"I've actually spoken to Portuguese whalers," Mister F. said, "men that hunt whales and kill whales for a living. None of those men had ever seen a giant squid, alive, that is."

Now, squeaking sounds, as corks twisted loose – all by themselves – from the necks of those specimen jars.

"But those men told me that just before a sperm whale dies, he breaches, and he vomits up huge chunks of giant squid." Mister F. made a loud, retching sound.

"Gross," someone said. Other kids laughed.

One after another, the corks fell to the floor. And then Mister Fishback's specimens escaped from their glass prisons, oozing, undulating, or just plain slopping out of those specimen jars and then either sliding down the wall or just letting go to hit the floor with wet plopping sounds.

"Just imagine," Mister Fishback said.

I was way ahead of him. Whole creatures and parts of other creatures inched and slid across the floor to gather, twitching and convulsing, at the feet of their master, their ringleader, staring up at Mister Fishback in wrinkly, long dead but well-preserved adoration.

21

Then, in low, gargling voices, those specimens began to sing "Sixteen Men on a Dead Man's Chest."

As Mister Fishback lectured on, I sat with Mihn, not blinking and wishing I could get this scene on film. It was so freaky that it was beautiful.

I jumped when the bell rang. But after my Steve-O-Scopic break from harsh reality, I felt a lot better. *Bettah*, that is.

Mister Fishback had also lost track of time. His pale, crooning brood had returned to their specimen jars. "Have an awesome break!" he said.

# Chapter Four

Seventh period. The last period before Spring Break. Mister Kaufman taught sociology – and driver's education on the side. Every Friday, he showed the most shocking and bloody films he could find, films with titles like *Highway of Agony*, *Blood on the Windshield*, and *Signal Thirty*.

These days, I've convinced myself that Mister Kaufman meant well, and I think he probably didn't know that my twin sister, Stephanie, had been killed by a drunk driver a few years earlier. But at the time, I hated Mister Kaufman for rubbing my nose in all that suffering, and I hated him for forcing me to remember things without any chance to escape into my imagination. Steve-O-Scope wasn't an option in Mister Kaufman's class because he always walked up and down the rows of desks, making sure we were awake and watching the action and soaking in every horrible, gory second. Thing is, I didn't even drive yet.

Today's film was a real gut twister: *Senior Skip Day*, thirty grainy minutes of amateur acting and real footage of twisted car metal and teenage body parts.

*"There would be no graduation ceremony for these seniors, no open coffins at their funerals, either."*

The film concluded with a slow zoom in to The Grim Reaper himself, surrounded by swirling, dry ice fog. It was a pretty cool effect, but for a terrible, flickering moment, I saw the Reaper wrap his rattling, skeletal fingers around Stephanie's throat, slowly choking her as she stared at me with pleading eyes.

That happened with Steve-O-Scope, sometimes. It got away from me.

The film ended, the bell rang, and I snapped out of it.

I went to my locker and tossed a copy of *Moby Dick* in my gym bag along with my dirty, musty PE clothes. At long last, Spring Break had officially started. Not only would there be no school tomorrow or Sunday, but there would be no school all of the following week. I planned on spending my vacation working on *Epoch Lost*, hanging out with Ken and Mihn and, of course, writing those two pages for Ms. Ellerath.

It should have been an exciting, exhilarating time. A time to celebrate. But I had been hurt and humiliated and I couldn't help but wonder why I couldn't have my own private movie theater where Pam Grier and I could watch *King Kong* and *The Valley of Gwangi* all day – and maybe rub noses during the trailers.

Real life was just hard, that's all. Things went wrong. Good people died. People threw oranges at you. And there wasn't much you could do about it, except escape into your head for a little while and hope you'd be able to come back out when things blew over.

I closed my locker and went outside. There weren't many bikes left in the rack. I unlocked my old three speed.

"How's your eye?" It was Mister Fishback. His British racing bike had leather saddle bags on either side of the rear wheel. I wondered again if Mister F. knew that I daydreamed – if he could tell, somehow, that I made movies in my mind. I wondered if he daydreamed about the deep, blue-green sea and all its amazing, underwater life. Fishback-Vision?

And I wondered if Julie Smith ever escaped into a fantasy world where she didn't need that metal brace. 70 mm Julie-Rama?

Maybe there was a whole underground culture of daydreaming oddballs out there – just like me. Maybe we could get together, support each other, trade daydreams, even, and keep each other from slipping over the edge and getting trapped in our own imagination. "Sorry about what happened at lunch today," Mister Fishback said.

"I'll be all right." I should have thanked Mister Fishback for protecting me during fifth period, but I didn't. "Can I ask a marine biology question?"

"Of course. Sure."

"Scientifically speaking," I asked, "why would a whale be white?"

"Like Moby Dick?"

Mister Fishback was on to me. "Right," I said.

"Believe it or not, I've seen pictures of albino whales," Mister Fishback said. "True albinos have pink eyes, though, and I don't recall Melville writing anything about Moby Dick having pink eyes."

"Me, neither."

"A white whale like Moby Dick would be incredibly rare. Maybe Melville made him white so he would stand out from all the other whales."

Made sense, but could I stretch that into two pages?

"I never could finish that book," Mister Fishback said. "That's why I majored in science. Not a lot of symbolism."

"OK," I said. "Well, have a good break."

"You, too."

Then we got on our bikes and rode off in opposite

directions.

I lived with Ma and Dad in a two story Victorian-style house on Desdemona Street, just above Roddy Bay. The bike ride home was downhill most of the way, so I could coast without using my brakes very much. But about half-way home, I had to swerve to avoid a crowd of boys that had gathered to watch a girl fight. The girls were pulling each others' hair and cussing a lot, and the boys were laughing and not doing anything to stop the brawl. It was like one of Ma's scrum matches – but less organized, and without a cash prize for the winner.

*"Primitive female passion, unleashed and on naked display!"*

I crossed the Coast Highway without having to stop and coasted the rest of the way home. I parked my bike outside Dad's shop. Just as I went inside, it started to rain. It always rains during Spring Break, but it doesn't rain hard, like in the winter, or for very long.

And then I stretched out on the couch, listened to the rain, tried not to think about my sore eye or terrible car wrecks that killed nice people, and took one of the best naps of my entire life. I probably wouldn't have slept so soundly if I knew that a tsunami of creepiness was headed my way.

# Chapter Five
## That Night

A huge reptile stood above the still-cooling sea, slowly chewing on moss and beach grass.

*"The mighty beast towered above his elemental world!"*

In real life, Brachiosaurs were about forty feet high and eighty feet long. My Brachiosaurus, on the other hand, was about eight inches high and a foot long – and made of gray-green modeling clay. Its eyes were painted BB's. Its teeth were chips of Ivory Soap. I had textured the Brachiosaurs' skin with crumpled tin foil, and had carved in other details – lines and wrinkles and scars – with a king crab claw that I'd saved from a left over bowl of Ma's *ciappino*. I was pretty proud of that critter.

The dinosaur's miniature surroundings were rocks and sifted beach sand, glued to a piece of plywood and elevated to camera level on a cardboard box. My camera was mounted on a tripod, along with two flood lamps.

This was a double exposure shot. I had already filmed thirty seconds of Roddy Bay with the top half of the lens masked off. At the end of that half minute, I rewound the film for a second run through the camera. Now, as I animated the Brachiosaurus, the bottom half of the lens was covered, so if I had done everything right, the result would be a believable combination of live action and animation, sure to impress the film school professors and get me into their program.

Dad was on his side of the shop, adjusting the brakes on a '62 VW bug. The garage door was open. I could smell gasoline and brake fluid, but that was OK, since after all, petroleum is actually dead dinosaur squeezin's. Behind me, the fan in Ma's meat freezer turned on and off every few minutes.

Kneeling on the cold cement floor, I leaned in and moved the Brachiosaur's lower jaw an eighth of an inch to the right. I sat back, being careful not to bump into the tripod, and touched – ever so lightly – the shutter release. A single frame of film was exposed. Then I checked another square on a sheet of graph paper. That's how I kept count of the number frames I had already shot, and how many I had to finish.

I moved the jaw to the left this time. Click. Check.

Clay jaw to the left. Click. Check. Eighteen frames of film equaled one brief second of animation. This thirty-second scene required 540 separate exposures. Even though it was tempting, you could never, never just run off a few extra frames to show the animal standing still, as if considering what to do next, or maybe resting. That was a lazy, unprofessional thing for an animator to do. I had been working on this scene for a week. It was almost done. Just fifty-three frames to go.

Licking my fingers and then rubbing them together so that I wouldn't leave my fingerprints in the clay, I moved the jaw to the left again. Then I pushed the head of the Brachiosaurus upward, maybe one sixteenth of an inch, beginning a series of movements that would show the dinosaur watching, searching for something. An offspring, maybe, or a mate.

BAP! I got whacked for the second time that day, but in the back of the neck this time. Something icy

28

cold slid down the back of my shirt and made me shiver.

Ma: "I warned you! No more dinosaurs in the refrigerator!"

I didn't have to look. Ma was standing in the door behind me, hands on her hips, wearing her Seaport Slammers jersey, with her blond hair in Viking braids.

I reached into the waistband of my underwear – where my frozen clay Dimetrodon had come to rest – and retrieved the little beast. It was still frosty, and the back fin was in good shape. "You didn't say anything about the freezer."

"Don't play mind checkers with me, sticky-foot!" Ma headed back to the house. "And if some sorry son of a steeple jack throws another orange at you, you juke him right in the voice box!"

"Right, Ma." Let me explain this refrigerator/freezer business. Hollywood's great dinosaur wranglers started with a jointed metal skeleton, to which they added foam rubber muscles and then a skin of scaly latex. That armature gave the model support.

My clay creatures, on the other hand, especially the bigger, heavier ones – your Ceratopsids and Sauropods, for example – tended to sag under their own weight, especially when hot lights were pointed at them. So I propped them up by inserting clothes hanger wire or wooden dowel sticks into their legs and up inside their bodies. It also helped to keep my monsterpieces in the refrigerator between scenes, the same way human actors rest in their air conditioned trailers, because the cold kept them in shape.

All well and good. But a few weeks earlier, during Bunco night at our house, one of Ma's roller derby partners, Mrs. Foote, went to Ma's avocado kitchen for a cold can of Olympia beer. When she opened the avocado refrigerator and happened to notice an Allosaurus, half-hidden behind a bowl of Ma's clam dip and grin-wheezing like that cartoon dog, Muttly, she jumped back, yelled something about an iguana, and then let out a loud and long scream of terror.

It was a good scream, too. Fay Wray would've been proud of it. I'm pretty proud of the fact that Mrs. Foote thought my Allosaurus was real, because that's what special effects are all about: fooling your audience, pulling off an illusion, making people ask, How Did They Do That?

But Ma wasn't impressed. At all. And the next morning, she delivered an ultimatum. OK, a threat: "If I find another crittersaurus in my refrigerator, I will jam you up!"

Ma wasn't what you'd call a pushover. She said what she meant and she meant what she said. Just like John Wayne. Ma had grown up in a fishing family. Her dad, my Grandpa, was a strong man with hands like cold granite from decades at sea, and I don't remember ever seeing him smile. Not even once. Not even when we watched *Abbott and Costello Meet the Mummy* one time while he was babysitting me.

Ma didn't understand my creature obsession. It just wasn't practical, as far as she was concerned. Neither was film school, or making a career out of playing with dinosaurs and monsters. But Ma had her soft side, too. Whenever we went fishing, for example, Ma always clubbed whatever we'd caught with one, efficient and very humane whack to the head. And she never pulled the trigger on a deer or an elk unless she knew she could bring it down with a single, merciful shot.

Oh, well. At least that frozen Dimetrodon was one

of the smaller prehistoric species. And it hadn't smacked into the lights or my little beach set, thereby ruining hours and hours of work.

I took some comfort in the knowledge that Ray Harryhausen, the frame by frame sorcerer behind *One Million Years BC*, and *The Valley of Gwangi* got a whipping when he was a boy, after cutting up the fur collar on one of his own mother's coats and using it to make a Wooly Cave Bear. Or so the story goes.

*"Everybody has to pay their Mesozoic dues!"*

I thought maybe I'd recall the Dimetrodon incident during some future awards acceptance speech, embarrass Ma a little. That would show her.

Back to work. Jaw to the left. Head forward just a little more. An hour later, my Brachiosaurus had abandoned his search, and was ready to exit the scene, stage right. How do you make a dinosaur walk? Two-legged creatures are relatively easy. You move one leg forward five or six times, taking a frame for each pose, and then you move the other leg. It's harder with four-legged animals, though. First, you pull one of the front legs forward a millimeter or two, and snap a frame, another, another. Then you move both that same front leg – and the opposite rear leg. Front leg, opposite rear leg. Front leg, opposite rear leg.

Eventually, that front leg stays where it is, the rear leg catches up, and then you start in on the opposite front leg. It's not easy. You have to remember which leg, which side of the body. And at the same time, your dinosaur's head and neck has to rock backwards and forwards as it walks, like a camel, and the tail has to sway from side to side, not just drag on the ground like a big wet rope. Everything has to move together as a whole, work in synch. That's how Harryhausen's creatures moved, constantly shifting weight, each hairy arm or scaly leg or suckered tentacle in constant, coordinated, synchronized motion. That's how real animals move.

Imagine how difficult it had been for Mister Harryhausen to animate that seven headed hydra in *Jason and the Argonauts*. And there were no retakes, no do-overs. If Ray didn't get it right, if he accidentally bumped the hydra or the camera, he had to start all over again.

A good animator had to concentrate, shut the rest of the world out, even if you'd had a bad day and been hit by a flying orange – and even if Pam Grier wanted you to rub her feet after a long day of kicking honky butt. That degree of concentration was easier for me than for most people, I think. Sometimes I lost all track of time out there in Dad's shop, bending clay necks and curling clay tails and tapping that shutter button. I was in my own universe, a safe place that ran by my rules, my logic, and my own sense of justice. Sometimes, without realizing it, I even talked to myself.

"Coulda been worse," I said. "Ronny coulda thrown a Hermiston apple at me." Hermiston apples, grown in eastern Oregon, are delicious, but larger than most apples, and harder than oranges. You wouldn't want to get hit in the face with one.

"That's a positive way to look at it." Dad was standing behind me, cold Oly in his hand. I wasn't sure if he had been there for ten seconds, or ten minutes, but if he had heard me talking to myself, he didn't let on. "How's it going, Junior?" Dad never called me by my name.

"Slow, but steady." I stared at the Brachiosaurus and committed its next set of movements to memory, just in case this was going to be a long conversation.

Which was likely.

Dad had a gut, a five o'clock shadow even an hour after he'd shaved, and he smiled a lot, showing the gap between his front teeth. He'd kept his Navy crew cut and had since added rockabilly sideburns. "Was that Ma, yelling?"

"Who else?" Of course, Dad had been yelled at even more than me. Ma had known him longer, after all. But she had only hit Dad once, when a mouse got in the house and ran up Dad's pants leg, making him scream and dance around until Ma grabbed the wooden cutting board that I'd made in shop class and whacked him in the zipper with it, killing the mouse and bringing Dad to his knees in pain.

Dad started to say something, but then he stopped. "Just a sec." He jogged to the open door, turned, and made a face.

"Hang on," I said, to the Brachiosaurus. We waited.

Dad cut a long, woodwind quality fart. Then he returned. "Excuse me." At least he was polite about it. I couldn't help but wonder if Willis O'Brien, all alone in a curtained corner of RKO studios, had ever cut the cheese between frames of the Kong/Pteranodon fight back in 1932.

Dad burped beer through his nose hairs. "Let's see that eye."

I tilted my head in Dad's direction and took off my mad scientist specs.

"You got a good shiner, there," Dad said.

"And a cut on my nose."

"Those Behrs are all sorry toad billiards, every last one of 'em." Ma didn't let Dad cuss, so he'd invented his own swear words: Torque bag. Chill spin. Fizz kidney. "Ronny's dad is in the crowbar hotel, you know." That meant jail.

"Ken might get kicked off both the wrestling team and the chess team," I said.

"Just because he punched Ronny Behr in the face?" Dad liked Ken. Sometimes they talked about cars. Sometimes Dad tried to talk to me about cars, too, but I just didn't know anything about engines and brake lines and pistons. "They should give Ken extra credit points. Anyways, I didn't mean to interrupt, Junior. I just wanted to know if you wanted to go crabbin' tomorrow, just the two of us. I've got some turkey necks thawing out."

"Old Jetty?" I asked.

"No better place to hunt the elusive Dungeness crab."

"Sure."

"I'll leave you two alone, then." Dad went back to work.

Me, too.

An hour later, the Brachiosaurus cleared the frame with one final, twelve frame, two-thirds of a second flick of his long clay tail.

# Chapter Six

I shut off the lights, unscrewed the camera from the tripod, and called it, as they say in the motion picture business, a wrap. I was beat.

It was always important for me to quit an hour or so before bedtime, take a break, calm down a little, and get dinosaur roars and movie voices out of my head. If I didn't try to rest my brain, I would toss and turn with nightmares about melting clay and not remembering how many frames I'd clicked off.

I placed my exhausted Brachiosaurus on the window sill to cool. Light spring rain started tapping on the other side of the glass.

Then I went in the house and passed through the family room. Dad was in his recliner, watching a news story on TV, something about a Chinese nuclear test. Ma sat on the couch, oiling her skate wheels and listening. I went to Ma's avocado kitchen to call Ken and make sure he was all right. I dialed his number from memory.

Ken lived in a swayback mobile home with his grandmother and his dad – who was usually gone, fishing and crabbing up in Alaska.

"Hello?" Ken's grandmother was Aleutian, I think. I had never met her. She always sounded tired on the phone.

"Is Ken there, please?"

"Just a moment."

"Thank you." I could hear "More than a Feeling" by Boston on the other end of the line. I liked that song. When people think of the seventies, they think of throbbing, soulless disco. But there was a lot of great music in the seventies: Bob Seger. Fleetwood Mac. Lots of good R&B, too.

Ken answered. "Hello?"

"How you doing, big guy?"

"I'm all right."

"I'm sorry you got in trouble," I said. "I'm such a wuss. I'm the one that got hit in the face. I should've punched Ronny." As I said the words, I felt like a dope. Of course, Ronny would've wiped up the cafeteria floor with me. "Is your grandmother mad?"

"Nah." Ken sighed. "Granny knows the deal."

"I'm going crabbing with Dad tomorrow morning. You want to go with us?"

"No, thanks." I think Ken was uncomfortable when he was around Dad and me because Ken's own dad was always gone. "Let's go to Don's when you get back. I'll buy."

"You always buy."

"I'm well-funded."

Then I heard claws scratching on a linoleum floor, and what sounded like the crash and clang of pots and pans and then Ken's grandmother yelling in her language.

*"It was the sound of terror unleashed!"*

Ken had a pet ferret that had been smashed dead by a logging truck. Ken's grandmother had actually sewn and bandaged and prayed the beast back to life. The poor thing still limped, and his right eye stuck out and moved independently of the left one. You could see a ring of suture scars around the base of his skull, and inside that circle, all of the hair had fallen out. The ferret's name had been Toby, but after being brought back from the dead we started calling him Zombie, or

36

just Zomb.

"Gotta go." Ken hung up.

"Thanks . . ." I hung up, went upstairs, stood in front of Stephanie's room, and put my hand on the door.

"Hey, Steph."

Ma had kept Steph's room exactly the way it was on the day she died. Sometimes, when Ma had one of her bad headaches, she slept in Steph's bed.

I never went in there, though. Neither did Dad. I don't know about Dad, but I didn't go into Steph's room because I was afraid that I would actually see her again – in the photographs I knew were in there, and in my memory – and that in order to cope, my Steve-O-Scopic imagination would kick into a psychotic, irreversible hyper spin, and suck me down into an alternative reality that I wouldn't be able to climb out of. Or something like that.

"Had a rough day, Steph. Ronny Behr hit me in the face with an orange. Now I have a black eye, and a cut nose because of my glasses. I'll be OK, though." I didn't know what else to say. I wanted to go inside, but I was afraid. "Night, Steph. Talk to you tomorrow."

Just down the hall, my own bedroom was small and cozy. I had a small, iron frame bed, a window that looked out over Roddy Bay, and a funky driftwood desk with a Zenith radio on it. I liked to think that Jim Hawkins, the kid in *Treasure Island*, had a bedroom like mine, up on the second floor of the Admiral Benbow Inn.

I opened the window just a little, letting in the cool, rain-cleaned air, weak moonlight, and the gentle rising, falling rush of Roddy Bay. I took off my shoes and socks and jeans. Then I got under the thick quilt that my grandmother had made and started flipping through *Moby Dick*, hoping to figure out the whale's pale pigmentation.

As I read about Queequeg, the tattooed cannibal, trying to sell a shrunken head in New Bedford, Ma came in with a grilled cheese sandwich on sourdough bread and a small glass of tomato juice with a shot of Worcestershire sauce in it.

Ma never knocked. She just came on in. I'm pretty sure she wanted to catch me at something.

"Thanks, Ma." I thought maybe the grub was her way of apologizing for throwing that Dimetrodon and yelling at me.

"You spill anything on Grandma's quilt, you're cold meat, you hear me?"

"OK, Ma."

She left. I read and I ate until I got drowsy. Then I turned out the light, and turned on my old glowing Zenith – but not so I could hear another Jim Croce or Doobie Brothers song.

*"Tonight:*
*Continued rain. Possibility of thunderstorms."*

It was a lady's voice. I still don't know who it actually was on the coast radio station, broadcasting weather conditions for the fishermen, but her voice had a low, lilting quality. I had turned that voice into Pam Grier's voice.

*"Tomorrow:*
*Early morning fog."*

Sometimes I saw Pam climbing out of Roddy Bay and looking like a bronze-skinned Venus. Sometimes she came to me, fresh from whatever righteous fight, that proud nose of hers beaded with sweat that was as pure as Oregon rain. Tonight, though, Pam stood next to my bed, wearing a fluffy white bathrobe after a long, hot shower. Pam let that robe drop, and the moonlight highlighted the strong curves of her steaming body. And that warrior nose. When she got under Grandma's quilt with me, her body was warm against mine. We rubbed noses for a long time. When we kissed and I tasted cinnamon in her mouth. Then we made love.

*"Rain in the afternoon.*
*Strong winds and high waves after midnight — sucka."*

Those winds and waves would bring something with them. Something huge and scary and mysterious.

I drifted off, and had another of my weird dreams. Sometimes, I dream in Technicolor. Sometimes, I dream in grainy black and white. I dream in Panavision most of the time, but every so often, my dreams are small and rounded off at the edges like a TV screen.

That night, I dreamed that Ahab finally killed Moby Dick, and then, with nothing to do, he opened up a chain of seafood restaurants and starred in the funniest, most bizarre TV commercial you never saw. In fact, I laughed so hard in my sleep that I woke myself up.

Dreams and movies . . .

# Chapter Seven
## Early Saturday Morning

Most high school boys would've slept in after a night of intense, nose to nose, Pam Grier sex. Not me. I was ready to hit Old Jetty with Dad and bag us some crabs.

I wasn't what you'd call an outdoorsman. Neither was Dad. Fishing and hunting and camping were more Ma's thing. But crabs, at least as far as Dad was concerned, were a different story. Lobsters, too. Shrimp. Crawdads. Anything with pinching claws. When Dad was a young surfer, living down in La Jolla, California, someone had dared him to stick his bare foot into a bucket of fresh caught crabs. Dad won the dare, but lost his little toe nail forever, and he had been on a quest to kill and eat crustaceans ever since – just like Captain Ahab I guess, but on a smaller, less crazy scale.

We always drove up the Summit for breakfast first, and Dad always let me drive his '71 VW bus because there weren't very many logging trucks on the road at that early hour.

Otis' Electric Kitchen was the only restaurant with food anywhere close to being as good as Ma's. It was a quiet kind of place, right on the river, with strong wooden chairs so that loggers and hunters – river men that wore beards and camouflage – could sit back and tell you all about their adventures. There were pictures on the walls of people you knew and the fish they had caught and the elk they had killed. Saw blades with

40

landscapes painted on them. Antlers, big enough to be prehistoric. And you could buy bait there.

Dad and I always sat in the same booth, under a signed picture of Bill Schonely, voice of the Portland Trailblazers and inventor of the phrase "Rip City!"

"How's the eye, this morning?" Dad asked.

"It only hurts when I use it." I wanted to tell Dad about the funny Captain Ahab commercial, but I couldn't remember all the details any more.

We always ordered the same thing: Pan-fried elk sausages. A side of fried potatoes. Black molasses toast with lots of butter. And black coffee that we sipped like men and winced as if we didn't even like the stuff.

"Why is Moby Dick white?" I asked. "It's for a homework assignment."

Dad thought for a second. "Maybe Moby Dick is white because he's actually a ghost of all the whales that were ever killed for their oil."

That sounded pretty cool.

I didn't say anything to Dad, but Ronny Behr's grandfather was also eating breakfast at Otis' that morning – just a few tables away. He was a large man, in his fifties, maybe older. He wore a flannel shirt beneath his overalls, steel toe work shoes, and an old pair of safety glasses. I did my best not to look in his direction.

After breakfast, Dad let me drive back down the summit to the Coast Highway and then way out to Old Jetty.

Seaport had two jetties. New Jetty, at the north end of town, was a strip of round black boulders that stretched a thousand feet out into the sea. It had been built by the Army Corps of Engineers in the 1920's, so it wasn't exactly new. Lots of people went crabbing

41

and fishing off of New Jetty.

Old Jetty, down to the south, wasn't even half as long as New Jetty. Wooden pylons and support beams had been added onto a natural outcrop of jagged, wave-carved rock, and they stuck out against the gray sky like the ribs of some dead sea beast. Nobody knew who built Old Jetty. Indians, maybe. Or Vikings. A Japanese freighter, the *Eiko Maru*, sank with all hands a half mile off Old Jetty in the fifties, and some people said that on cold foggy nights, you could hear Japanese voices out in the dark. Ghost voices. It was Dad's and my favorite crabbing spot.

By now, the sun had cracked the Summit. The offshore breeze was damp and a little chilly. Old Jetty reached out into the fog until you couldn't see the end of it. As usual, Dad and I had the whole thing to ourselves. It would be just the two of us – unless some Japanese skeletons decided to climb out of the water, that is, climb up onto the rocks, and ruin our day.

"Your time has come, crabs!" Dad hauled two crab rings out of the bus. "Prepare yourselves for the great boiling inevitable!" He laughed. "Sounds like the name of some hippy band, huh, Junior?"

"What does?"

"The Great Boiling Inevitable." Dad hated hippies. He said they had ruined surfing with all their dope and laziness.

We climbed up on the wet stones. I must admit, Dad was still pretty agile, jumping from one big rock to the next without a misstep. He wasn't as fast as me, though. Too bad rock hopping wasn't a sport, because I would have been a jock for sure. But we both knew to be careful on the jetty and pretty much anywhere near the ocean. Bad stuff happens if you aren't careful.

*"The sea punishes those who do not respect her!"*

It wasn't long before Dad and I were out far enough into the fog that we couldn't see the beach anymore. The gray ocean rose and fell on both sides of us. Waves broke against the jetty, and we could feel the impact come up through the rocks and wood and into our feet and legs. I've always been amazed by the power of wind, water, and tide.

Black rock. White fog. Gray ocean. It was like a scene from a movie made before color film. Or maybe one of those black and white European movies they show on PBS that always ended with the word "Fin," instead of "The End." We found our usual crabbing spot, a slab of flat rock between two pylons that was just high enough to be dry most of the time, but still close to the water.

How do you catch crabs? You tie soup bones or fish heads or turkey wings – the older and stinkier, the better – into the netting of your crab ring. You attach a long rope to your crab ring. Then you throw your crab ring into the water. And then you wait. After ten minutes or so, you pull up your crab ring and hopefully, you will have captured two or three Dungeness crabs, the best eatin' crabs in the world.

How do you cook Dungeness crabs? First, you ask your Ma to boil them in salty water until they turn red. Next your Dad cracks the crabs open and pulls out all the white, clean, steamy meat. Then your Ma will make her world-famous crab muffins – crab meat and melted cheese on an English muffin. Or her crab Louie salad with black olives. Or coleslaw with crab meat. Or *ciappino*. Of course, if you're impatient, or really hungry, or both, you can just cook the crabs right there on the beach and then crack the legs and claws with your fingers and teeth and dip the pieces

43

into melted butter.

Right now, Dad and I were in the waiting stage of the crab catching process.

Sometimes, Dad faked an interest in dinosaurs and monster movies. "I guess there was a time when there were some big, scary critters out there."

"Megalodon." I half whispered the name, and tried to remember details of Mister Fishback's lecture on the species.

"Mega what? Is that one of those deep water fish that explode when they come to the surface?"

"Megalodon was a prehistoric shark. It was like a Great White, but bigger."

"Bigger? How big? Big as the shark in *Jaws*?" Dad did a few CHUN CHUN CHUN CHUN notes from that movie's soundtrack.

"Megalodon was eighty feet long," I said. "Maybe even longer."

Dad whistled. "Man! That's a Sharkasaurus Rex."

*Cool monster name*, I thought. "Mister Fishback thinks that maybe Megalodon isn't extinct at all, that there are still some of them alive today."

"You like that Mister Fishback, don't ya, Junior?"

"He's my favorite teacher." Lightning flickered on the far horizon. Dull thunder followed. I had to make a conscious effort not to imitate Mister Fishback's accent. "A few years ago, a fisherman in Australia found a shark tooth in his net. It was five inches long. The tooth of a twenty-foot great shark is two inches long."

Dad made a quick calculation. "So a five-inch tooth came from a shark that was fifty feet long."

"Yep," I said. "Just imagine."

Lightning again. Thunder.

"When great whites get really big," Dad said, "they

get fat and butt crack ugly. They lose that streamlined, torpedo look. A fifty foot shark would be one nasty-lookin' son of a buck." He shivered. Maybe it was the cold air. Then again maybe not.

As I looked out into the fog, a triangle, blacker even than the jetty rock, rose from the white and gray, first two, then five, and then ten feet high. It was the dorsal fin of the extinct Sharkasaurus Rex. When I realized how impossibly huge the fish beneath that fin must be, I felt weak, unable to move or speak.

*"The sea's worst nightmare had returned from extinction, and it was hungry!"*

The fin swerved, cut toward the jetty, toward Dad and me. Then it plunged. Disappeared. I took off my mad scientist glasses and closed my eyes and I waited for the behemoth to breach, surge up out of the ocean, and then chomp Dad and me to death.

I waited a little longer. Then, I opened my eyes, put my specs back on. Nothing. Silence. I still had my arms and legs and head. But I was overwhelmed by that I'm being watched feeling.

Sure enough, lightning revealed, just beneath the surface, the Sharkasaurus Rex, its gigantic features bending and shifting under the water like a reflection in a fun house mirror. Rows of serrated, triangular teeth, set in a gaping mouth. Lifeless eyes staring right at me. Flaring, flexing gills. It was a terrifying – and butt crack ugly – thing to see. And for one dizzying second, I felt as if I wasn't going to get out of this one, that maybe the giant shark was real.

*"Only one thing could save them from the very maw of Hell!"*

Dad farted, and the Sharkasaurus sank out of sight. Nothing like the sudden release of pent-up intestinal gas to bring you back to reality.

"Excuse me." Dad got up, stretched, was about to pull the crab trap. Then he stopped and peered out into the fog, and I think maybe he remembered what I'd said about monster sharks still being out there. He turned. "You want to get it, Junior?"

Another flash of white light. Thunder, still miles out to sea. But closer than before. Dad and I both jumped a little.

"Storm's comin'," Dad said. "Big one."

Something else was on the way, too. Something with teeth. And tentacles.

*"It was a deep-ocean horror, straight out of a sea captain's fever dream!"*

# Chapter Eight

It started to rain, and we'd snagged enough crabs for dinner, so we packed up the bus and started for home.

Dad took the wheel this time. "What's the deal between you and Ronny Behr, anyways? Is it because of a chick?" Dad sounded hopeful – about me maybe being interested in a girl, a real girl, that is. He didn't know about Pam Grier, and I wasn't about to fill him in.

I decided to tell Dad about The Cyclops Incident, instead. "When I was in eighth grade I brought a Cyclops to school."

"Something you made?"

"It looked a lot like the Cyclops in *The Seventh Voyage of Sinbad*, but with a face like Richard Nixon."

"That's funny."

"Anyways, when Ronny saw my clay Cyclops he brought his hand down right on top of its head and slammed it almost flat."

"That was a mean thing to do."

"The Cyclops got the last laugh, though. I had stuck some 1/8-inch dowel sticks into his legs to help keep him standing upright. The pointy ends went right into Ronny's hand. He had to have a tetanus shot and stiches and a big bandage. His hand got infected, anyway. It turned all purple and black and they had to amputate part of his middle finger."

"Whoa!"

Just then, an elk, a big bull, appeared on our side

47

of the road. Dad pulled over, stopped the bus, put it in neutral, and turned on the hazard lights in case someone came up behind us. "Good thing Ma isn't here," he said.

The elk crossed in front of us, lit up in our headlights, moving slowly, completely unafraid, and as breathtaking as any landscape.

"Good thing." I studied the animal's movements, the way its weight shifted as it walked, the way it raised its great head as it sniffed the cool air.

And then the elk reached the other side of the road and disappeared into the trees as if it had never existed.

"Why did the elk cross the road, Junior?"

"I don't know, Dad. Why did the elk cross the road?"

Dad turned off the hazard lights and shifted into first gear. "Because something that perfect has the right to do whatever it wants."

That elk was perfect and beautiful and it was real, not some daydream or special effect.

# Chapter Nine
## That Afternoon

The sky was overcast, but it wasn't raining any more. I was waiting out in the driveway when I heard one of my favorite songs, "Werewolves of London" by Warren Zevon. You could always hear Ken's stereo before you saw his Thunderbird.

The big car turned onto Desdemona Street and up into our driveway.

"Howdy." Whenever Ken was behind the wheel, he wore a pair of old welder's goggles that made him look like a crazy Samoan scuba diver. "Did you catch any crabs?"

"Plenty." I rounded the front of the car.

"How is your mom going to fix 'em?"

I noticed that three fingers on Ken's Ronny-punching hand were taped together. "I don't know yet."

Mihn rode shotgun as usual. "I like crabs." He jumped out, held the door open for me, and I dove into the backseat. We had perfected these moves over many missions, and by now we were as efficient as any race track pit crew.

Zombie, in the back seat and glad to see me, jumped up to my shoulder.

Ken pulled a U-ber, and then we were off to our hangout – and the only fast food place in Seaport.

Don's Last Stand had a curving tile roof and snarling cement lions on both sides of the front door and had actually been a Chinese restaurant at one

49

time, back when Ma was in high school. In the intervening years, though, that same building had been a TV repair shop, a hardware store, and very briefly, before the cops shut it down, an herbarium. Whatever that is. That's the way things are on the Oregon Coast. Things always change, but in ways you never expect.

Don's was also the home of THE WORST CLAM CHOWDER ON THE OREGON COAST which, if you dared to order it, was actually Campbell's chicken and stars soup.

Ken whipped the wheel hard to starboard, piloted the T-Bird into our usual space, and parked. He turned to the back seat. "Zombie, stay!"

The ferret whined and hissed and that freaky eye rolled to the left and bounced a little and then came to a rolling rest at the bottom of the socket. Poor Zomb.

Ken pulled himself up and out of the Bird. Mihn got out and held the car door for me.

"I'll bring something back for you, Zombie," I said.

Zombie's tail, probably the only thing on him that hadn't been smashed, killed, and then repaired, whipped back and forth.

We went inside and sat at our favorite booth. Don, or Agent Orange, as we called him – but never to his face – was a scary-lookin' character with a rawboned, clean-shaven face, bushy eyebrows, and a shaved head. According to local myth and rumor, Don had actually been a spy of some type, assigned to one government agency or another, during the fifties and sixties. Either that, or a school bus driver. Don's restaurant was as clean and simple as a Marine Corps mess hall. The only decorative features were old-timey ceiling fans that Don might have stolen from some Saigon opium den – and a photograph of a group of

50

men, standing in a rice paddy with a water buffalo. One of the men in the photo could have been Don, but it was hard to tell since all the men's eyes were masked with black stripes in order to conceal their identity. That photograph lent at least some credibility to the spy rumor.

Retired – from whatever – now, Don wasn't the best cook, but his prices were low, and he didn't mind if you ate and then just sat for a while, talking with your best friends about whatever was on your mind that day. And you could buy bait there.

Best of all, Ronny Behr had been recently banned from Don's – after breaking in after hours, attempting to crowbar into Don's jukebox, and not knowing that Don was in the back room/commo bunker, working on some sinister project or another. Busted. Ronny was arrested, and spent the night in jail. His sentence was still pending.

"Welcome to Don's Last Stand." Don always said those words with all the sincerity of a kid being forced to apologize by his mom. "What'll it be, lads?"

"Hangtown Special." Ken rubbed his hands together. Everyone on the Oregon Coast knows that a Hangtown Fry is a kind of omelet made of eggs, cheddar cheese, fried oysters, bacon, and spinach. A Hangtown Special, on the other hand, is when you put all that between two very large hamburger buns. Ken invented it, apparently. "And a Mister Pibb."

"I should have known." Don never wrote down your order down. He was pretty accurate, but if he got something wrong, it was best not to argue with him. And if you found one of his eyebrow hairs in your fries, it was best to just let it go.

"Shrimp burger, fries, and a root beer, please." I had eaten a Hangtown Special once, at Ken's insistence. And once was enough for a life time. That thing sat immobile in my gut like lead ballast for an entire day.

Mihn ordered the fried shrimp basket with fries and lemonade.

"Got it." Don snapped his fingers and committed our orders to memory. "Be back in a few."

We were Don's only customers at the moment. "I have a great idea for a movie," Ken said. "You guys want to hear my pitch?"

"Thrill me," I said.

"The title alone will sell you. Pure exploitation genius."

"Lay it on us," Mihn said.

Ken hummed a few melodramatic notes, built to a crescendo. Then he cupped brutish hands on either side of his mouth and spoke in his deepest, most melodramatic voice – which always sounded to me like a cross between Orson Welles and Tony the Tiger: *They Saved Disney's Brain!*"

A second of stunned silence.

"Disney's brain?" I asked.

"Disney?" Mihn asked. "Walt Disney?"

Ken started in on a brief biography of Walt Disney. For Mihn's benefit, apparently.

But it was unnecessary. "I know who Walt Disney was," Mihn said. "My family lived in a relocation facility in Anaheim before we moved to Oregon."

"But did you know," Ken asked, "that Disney ordered his top animators to cut off his head after he died and then freeze it?"

"Freeze it? Mihn asked. "Why?"

"So that one day they could attach the frozen head to a healthy body," Ken said, "and bring Disney back to life. Just imagine the secret plans, the oaths of secrecy. The cover-ups."

"Disneygate!" I could see the opening scene of Ken's movie. It would be just like Citizen Kane, but with a Steve-O-Scopic twist.

Midnight, somewhere in the Magic Kingdom, well after closing time. The camera slowly cranes around the Jungle Cruise and under the monorail and past the Haunted Mansion and up to a high, lonely light burning in a window of the Sleeping Beauty Castle. Inside, Walt Disney lies under the window in a huge bed. As a low and creepy Bernard Herrmann version of "It's a Small World" plays on the soundtrack, Disney holds a ceramic Mickey Mouse figure in his hands, studying it, and remembering his past.

Close up: Disney's mouth and clipped mustache as he whispers the words, "Funicello."

Disney's hands fall to his sides. Mickey falls to the floor and breaks. A nurse comes rushing into the room. She checks Disney's pulse, finds that he has died, and pulls a sheet over his head. Then the nurse pulls a bell chord and a team of men, dressed in surgical gowns and carrying sharp surgical instruments, enters the room.

Eerie, I thought. And kinda cool. Maybe my Neanderthal friend was on to something, after all.

Ken had been relating details of his story to Mihn. "And then, Disney gets into an epic fight with the President Lincoln robot!"

"Who wins?" Mihn asked.

"Lincoln, of course!" Ken giggled and tapped his little feet under the table.

I had to step in. "Does your movie follow the rules?"

"Rules?"

"Rules. Even your cheapest, no budget sci-fi

53

monster movie has to follow some basic rules."

"Elucidate," Mihn said.

"OK," I said. "You need a hero. And you need a pretty girl."

"Makes sense, "Ken said. "I already have an actress in mind." He nudged Mihn.

"My sister will not be in your monster movie," Mihn said. "Sorry ass bomb!

I went on. "Your monster has to be hideous, terrifying. But sympathetic at the same time. And at the end, your monster has to go out in some dramatic, spectacular way – but only after teaching everybody some profound lesson."

Ken burped. "Such as….?"

"Man should not tamper with nature," I said. "That kind of stuff."

"I see."

"One last thing," I said. "And this is very important. You need lots of real-life film of tanks and police cars and helicopters."

"Why is that?"

"Cheap realism."

As Ken pondered these rules, a dad, a mom, and their two kids came in the front door. They sat down at a booth and started looking over Don's menu.

"Out of towners," I said.

"Tourists," Mihn said.

I looked outside. Sure, enough, there was a station wagon parked next to Ken's T-Bird and it had Idaho license plates on it.

We knew things were about to get interesting for the tourists. In the meantime, Ken had a riddle for us. "What did Captain Ahab say when he caught Moby Dick crying?"

"I don't know," I said. "What did Captain Ahab

say when he caught Moby Dick crying?"

"Quit your blubbering," Ken said. "Get it?"

Whenever Mihn laughed, it sounded like backwards-hiccups. "Very funny!"

I just shook my head.

Tourist Dad was the first to realize that there wasn't any Chinese food on the menu. No egg drop soup. No *chop suey*. Tourist Mom wasn't far behind, and started carping at her husband. Tourist Kids just sat there looking dopey.

"I love this," Ken said.

Tourist Dad sat up and looked around. Tourist Mom pointed to the kitchen and carped some more.

"Don't listen to her," I whispered. Pam Grier never nagged me like that. And that's the truth, Ruth.

Tourist Dad, who was probably beat and hungry, got up and walked over to the swinging saloon-style doors of Don's kitchen. "Excuse me?" There was no answer. "Excuse . . ."

Don suddenly appeared, trailing steam and smoke behind him like a character escaping Hell in some Italian opera, and the conversation started. "Welcome to Don's Last Stand. Can I help you?"

"Do you serve Chinese food here?"

"No." Don acted as if it was an odd and possibly stupid question.

"But this is a Chinese restaurant."

"It is?"

"There are lions outside."

"That's correct."

"So, this must be a Chinese restaurant."

"I don't follow your logic."

This went on for almost a minute before Tourist Dad gave up and herded Tourist Family back out to the car – with Tourist Mom griping all the way. We waited until their car pulled out of the lot before we broke out laughing.

We stopped laughing when Don brought our food.

Ken's Hangtown Special took up half the tray. It was cut in two sections, since no mere human could pick up the whole thing at once, and held upright by toothpicks.

"Will you be able to eat that thing with those bandaged fingers?" Don asked.

"Watch me." Ken used both hands to hoist half of his Hangtown Special up to his salivating mouth.

"No, thanks." Don headed back to the kitchen. "Let me know if you need anything else."

I squirted ketchup on my fries. Mihn stirred salt into his lemonade. That's how they like it in Vietnam, apparently.

Ken studied it for a strategic starting point, and then he took a massive first bite. It was like watching a killer whale chomp down on a harbor seal. Mihn and I both looked away.

I saw Zombie out in the car, up on the dashboard with his tongue hanging out and that loose eye rolling back and forth at the bottom of its socket. Poor Zomb.

*"Would such a beast ever know love?"*

We ate and we talked. Ken polished off his Hangtown Special, but I guess he was still hungry, because he grabbed several of Mihn's French fries and scarfed them down before Mihn could do anything.

Mihn took a calm, salty sip of his lemonade. "Help yourself, Ken."

After lunch, we piled back into Ken's T-Bird. I had managed to save a few fries for Zombie, and he snapped them up. It wasn't pretty.

"You're going to spoil that sorry beast," Ken said.

Thunder rumbled above Seaport.

Zombie growled.

# Chapter Ten
## Saturday Night

I had saved enough room for dinner: Ma's crab and cheese muffins. Ma killed the crabs as quickly and humanely as possible. As much as Dad hated crabs, he couldn't stand to watch 'em go into the pot. Neither could I. Once the crabs were cooked, though, Dad took over, cracking the claws and legs with a mallet and pulling the steaming white meat from the red shells with a metal walnut pick. Then Ma put the crab meat and some mild cheddar on English muffins and put them under the broiler just long enough to melt the cheese. Dad liked hot sauce on his. I think that was something he picked up in the Navy.

I set the table: Ma's home-baked bread. Pickled beets. Tea. And I always set a place for Steph.

As we ate in Ma's avocado kitchen, we heard it raining outside. Hard, now. And it felt good to be warm and dry, and eating our own good food.

"That black eye makes you look kinda tough," Dad said, "like you're one bad motor scooter."

Of course, Ma didn't agree. "Looks like rink rash, to me."

"Ask your mother about *Moby Dick*," Dad said.

"*Moby Dick*?" Ma gave me one of her don't-mess-with-me looks.

"It's for school," I said. "Why was the whale white? What does white represent?"

I was sure Ma was about to give me some sort of sarcastic answer, so I was surprised by what she said.

"Moby Dick was a symbol for justice. He killed Ahab and all the other whalers except for Ishmael because Ishmael didn't have as much whale blood on his hands, and then he sank the *Pequod* so it would never hunt whale again."

"Whoa!" I said. I was impressed. Could I get two pages out of Ma's idea?

Dad and I always took turns with the dishes. Tonight was my night. As I stood at the sink, rinsing plates, I studied Ma's collection of wooden sea captains on the window sill in front of me. Some were antiques, with dings and faded paint. Most had peg legs. They all looked like they were related – grandfathers, uncles, fathers and sons – all gathered together at some maritime souvenir reunion and waiting for me to finish up so they could grumble to each other about the things wooden sea captains grumble about, and maybe drink some rum.

*All carved out of wood*
*these ancient mariners stand*
*above soapy waves.*

I made sure Ma and Dad were in the family room. Then I asked the captains about Moby Dick's whiteness. After all, who would know better about whales and such? But there was no consensus.

After I finished up with the dishes, I played a few games of carrom with Ma and Dad. Ma made caramel corn. Then we watched *Portland Wrestling*. I never believed that Dutch Savage and the Von Steiger Brothers were actually duking it out – not even when I was a little kid. The fight scenes in *King Kong vs. Godzilla* were more realistic – and better choreographed – as far as I'm concerned. But it was fun to watch Ma rant and yell and jump up and down.

We watched the news. Then Ma and Dad went to bed, and it was just me and Pam Grier. Until midnight, that is, and my favorite TV show.

*Creature Feature*, sponsored by Les Schwab Tires, was one of those low-budget, monster movie programs, produced in Portland. Most of the movies on *Creature Feature* were old classics from the thirties, forties, and fifties, like *Son of Frankenstein. The Creature from the Black Lagoon.* There were some duds, too. *The Giant Claw. Attack of the Crab Monsters. King Kong* came on once a year.

The show always began with a night shot of a spooky old house, or more accurately, a cheesy cardboard model of a spooky old house. If you looked closely, you could see a tiny, rolled up newspaper on the roof above the doorway – as if thrown by a five-inch paperboy with a bad aim. I loved that little detail, and wondered if anyone else had ever caught it.

Pam and I settled in.

The TV camera zooms slowly in on that spooky old house. Eerie organ music. Wolves howling. Lap dissolve to: The interior of the spooky old house, all decked out with Victorian furniture, heavy drapes, and a stone fireplace. Dave the weatherman apparently made a few extra bucks on Saturday night, doing a pretty fair impression of Boris Karloff: "And now, here's the host of *Creature Feature*, Professor Ravenswort."

Then the star of the show appears, tall, gaunt and a little unhealthy-looking, holding a candelabra. He wears a black cape with a high, Dracula style collar. Old timey dark shades with hinges and blinders on the sides. And red, high top sneakers.

"Good evening, boys and ghouls." Professor

Ravenswort speaks in a loud, theatrical voice and he rolls his R's. "Welcome to another creeptastic, monsterific show!" The professor has his own fan club, his own newsletter, and he makes personal appearances at local shopping centers and movie theaters. "Tonight we present a true sci-fi classic, The *Beast from 20,000 Fathoms*!"

This low-budget masterpiece was Ray Harryhausen's first solo movie and the very first sleeping-dinosaur-reawakes-to-smash-things-and-eat-people movie ever made.

But before the movie starts, an ad for Les Schwab Tires, and after that, a campaign commercial for Tom McCall.

Mister McCall was the former two term governor of Oregon. If it wasn't for Mister McCall, our roads would be littered with pop bottles and beer cans, our beaches would belong to the highest bidder, and Oregon would basically be California. Mister McCall was a plainspoken poet and seemed to be an honest man. And now, after some time off, McCall was back on the campaign trail.

In the commercial, Mister McCall stands above the Columbia River. His gray-white hair blows in the wind, and the top button of his flannel shirt is buttoned. I always thought Mister McCall looked a little like Franklin Roosevelt. He had that same jutting lower jaw. "There is no such thing as a typical Oregonian," McCall says, "but we all share in a deep and abiding love for this place we call home."

I liked Mister McCall. So did my folks. So did just about everybody I knew.

"Once again, our home is being threatened by the twin scourges of corruption and greed, and I can no longer stand idly by. I hope you will join me in this historic cause."

The commercials ends, and the movie begins.

Somewhere north of the Arctic Circle, scientists detonate an atomic test explosion. An egghead watches from a safe distance and ponders the as yet unknown effects of these government experiments: "What the cumulative effects of all those atomic explosions and tests will be, only time will tell." Sure enough, the blast causes great icebergs to crumble and melt and rouse a Rhedosaurus – a four-legged hybrid of an alligator and a T. Rex, with lots of scales and claws and teeth – from its billion-year sleepy bye. Naturally, the old timer is a bit confused, cranky. And lonely. He heads for New York City to knock over buildings and eat cops and hopefully find a mate.

The high point of the movie, for me, at least, is when the Rhedosaurus hears the fog horn of an old-timey lighthouse, and then emerges from the sea, thinking and hoping that he's found love. Sorry, old bean. No such luck. When the dinosaur realizes he'd been stood up, he tears down the lighthouse. (If you look carefully, you can see that Mister Harryhausen actually animated tiny bricks, each one suspended on hidden wires, one frame at a time.) The two caretakers barely make it out alive.

The Rhedosaurus is eventually cornered within the twisting tracks of a Coney Island roller coaster, shot with a radioactive isotope, and then dies, after a lot of overly dramatic roaring and clawing.

Fantastic stuff. Definitely four stars in my book. And all the elements are there: A hero, a pretty girl, a spectacular climax. And lots of military stock footage.

But it was a good thing that I had already seen this movie. Because just about the time the Rhedosaurus came climbing up out of the Hudson River, thunder exploded right above our house like an H-bomb.

Upstairs, Ma yelled something. Then, Dad. The TV popped and went dark. The power was out. A second blast of thunder. Then, rain, lashing hard against the windows and the roof.

The folks came downstairs. Dad fired up a small gas lantern, went to the family room, put it on the floor next to him, and stood staring out the sliding glass doors. Ma went to her avocado kitchen and called one of her skate buddies. I joined Dad. Neither one of us said anything. Outside, Roddy Bay was darker than the flashing sky. Lightning glanced off the wave troughs and made the frothy breakers glow like green neon.

I'm sure Dad was worrying about wind and water damage to the house and trying to decide whether we should all pack up and head for higher ground. But I was imagining hundreds of great sea beasts – Plesiosaurs, Mosasaurs, and other dinosaurs – all appearing and then disappearing beneath the roiling surface of the sea. Gigantic shadows. Terrifying shapes. And I saw horrible flying things, their veiny wings turned momentarily transparent by lightning, flapping above the water searching for food, and sometimes being caught as food themselves.

That's what ocean life was like back then, I thought. Brutal. Unforgiving. Like in the Oz cafeteria, only a lot worse. When I closed my eyes, lightning lit up the veins in my eyelids.

*The sea is deep, still*
*No light can find its bottom*
*What is hiding there?*

The storm howled and roared. The wind made our

house on Desdemona Street creak like an old four-masted schooner. When I finally went upstairs, it was way late and still raining. I said goodnight to Steph, and then hit the sack. My Zenith wouldn't work, of course, so I had to listen to Pam on a little battery-powered transistor radio. Her voice sounded more distant than usual. And not very romantic at all.

*"Tonight and into Tomorrow:*
*High winds and very rough seas.*
*Winds at Sixty knots.*
*Wind waves at eighteen to twenty feet.*
*Strong possibility of fallen trees and downed power lines."*

Too tired for any Pam Grier nose rubbing, I fell asleep right away. I dreamed a sequel to *The Beast from 20,000 Fathoms*. In my dream, the Rhedosaurus had just flattened the lighthouse, leaving only Old Jetty standing. The two caretakers were up on the sand, in the dark, looking over the wreckage, panting and sweating and wondering how they would ever explain what had happened.

That's when Julie Smith, not Pam Grier, appeared, wearing a white dress that flowed in the wind behind her – and that metal neck brace.

As the caretakers watched, Julie walked over and around the lighthouse rubble and to the rocky end of Old Jetty where the dark sea churned on three sides of her. Julie was looking for her dinosaur. The dinosaur had come looking for her. They had just missed each other.

Julie turned away from the sea and began to weep and I felt sad for her.

# Chapter Eleven

## Sunday Morning

I woke up to the smell of frying baloney – which meant that the power was back on. I slid out from under Grandma's quilt so that I wouldn't have to make the bed, took a quick shower, and got dressed. The sun had already busted the Summit, but it was hidden behind thick gray and white clouds. It was still windy and raining, but not as severely as last night.

Downstairs, Dad was in Ma's avocado kitchen, cooking breakfast for the two of us, just like he did every Sunday. I checked the blackboard that we used to keep track of each other. The word CHURCH was written next to MA.

Saint Mary's by the Sea was a tiny fishermen's church with stone walls and stained glass windows and a children's choir. Every Sunday since Stephanie's funeral, even on bad weather Sundays like this one, Ma put on her best clothes and went to Saint Mary's.

Ma never went inside, though. She always sat on a stone bench behind the church and looked out over the ocean and listened as the congregation prayed and the choir sang. Ma said the kids always sounded like angels, singing in Heaven, and that every once in a while, she was sure, absolutely sure, that she could hear Steph's voice, too.

Sometimes, Ma came home really happy, and sometimes, you could tell she'd been crying, and on those Sundays, she would go up to Stephanie's room and lie down on the bed and wouldn't come down all day.

"Hungry?" Dad asked.

"And how," I said.

Then Dad and I ate our fried baloney and cheddar cheese sandwiches and we drank black coffee and made man faces and we watched old Warner Brothers cartoons on TV. We laughed and talked, but only if we felt like it, and we didn't talk about sad things.

Ma came home later that morning – in a happy mood – and when she told Dad that his little girl had been in fine voice today, Dad nodded his head and smiled and said he was glad.

It rained the rest of the morning and into the afternoon. The wind kicked up hard for a while. The power went out and came back on again. Four times. Since we couldn't depend on the power, Ma cooked dinner in the fireplace: deer steaks, baked potatoes, and fried fiddle head ferns. Good stuff.

After dinner, I washed dishes with the old sea captains. Then I went out to Dad's shop and tore down my Brachiosaurus, removing the teeth and eyes and the support sticks first and then smashing the whole thing down and rolling it into a big gray-green ball of clay.

Whenever I tore down a Brontosaurus or a Triceratops, I felt sorta sad, like I ought to have some sort of funeral. But whatever I killed would be recycled, reborn into something else. Strange, I know. I gave my creatures life, then I killed them, and then I gave them a new, different life. I could only imagine the off-the-wall, literary symbolism that Ms. Ellerath could read into the life/death/life process.

I could've started in on the baby Tyrannosaurs I needed for *Epoch Now*. But it was getting late, so I decided to call it a day. I went upstairs and put my hand on Stephanie's door.

"Ma says she heard you singing this morning," I said. "She said you sounded real good." There was nothing else to say. I knew Steph wanted me to come inside, but I didn't.

Then I went to my room, read about the giant squid in *Moby Dick*, and wondering if Mister Fishback knew about that chapter. Then I turned out the light and listened to Pam's voice.

*"Tonight:*
*West winds at fifteen to twenty knots.*
*Wind waves at twelve to fifteen feet.*
*Rain ending early tomorrow."*

Pam and I rubbed noses as lightning flashed on her brown skin and glistened in her 'Fro. Afterwards, I fell asleep and had another insane dream about being a Humphrey Bogart type detective with a peg leg, trying to track down a mysterious white whale, and not having any luck, sweetheart. Julie Smith was my wise cracking, gum snapping secretary. Imagine being a detective and not being able to find something as large and obvious as a whale.

Thinking back, I figure that just about the time I was having that dumb whale detective dream, something monstrous came ashore in Seaport.

*"The hideous monstrosity would pose a mystery as old as the sea itself!"*

# -Part Two-

"There she blows! There she blows! A hump like a snow-hill! It is Moby Dick!"
   — **Moby Dick, Herman Melville, 1851**

"UP FROM THE FORBIDDEN DEPTHS COMES A TIDAL WAVE OF TERROR!"
   – **Poster, *Monster From the Ocean Floor,* 1954**

"I dreamed I was in a Hollywood movie And that I was the star of the movie This really blew my mind."
   – **"Spill the Wine," War, 1971**

Oregonians don't tan.
They rust."
   – **Popular T–shirt, 1970's**

# Chapter Twelve

## Monday

Pam and I were hoping to sleep late on that first official, no school morning of Spring Break, 1978.

But no.

"Steve, your Vietnamese buddy is on the phone." Dad was outside my room, knocking on the door. Unlike Ma, he never came barging in, trying to catch me in the act. Us, that is.

"OK." Pam was still asleep, and I didn't want to bother her, so I just gave her a quick peck on the nose and reminded her to keep on keepin' on. Then I put on my jeans and my mad scientist glasses, went downstairs to Ma's avocado kitchen, and answered the phone. "Hello?"

"Hello, Steve." It was either really fun to talk on the phone with Mihn, or really annoying. He took phone rules very seriously. "This is Mihn."

"Hello, Mihn. How are you?"

"I'm fine, Steve. And how are you?"

"I am fine as well."

Silence.

"How can I help you this morning, Mihn?"

Now that we'd gotten past the formalities, Mihn could drop the bomb. "There is a dead monster on Ono Beach! No joking. During the storm last night, something ass big and very ass scary washed up on the beach. My mother heard it on the radio. You will never guess who found the monster. Mister Fishback, that's who!"

"Mister Fishback?"

"He is our fifth period marine biology teacher."

"I know who he is, Mihn."

"He discovered the monster. Can you believe that ass?"

Monster? Ono Beach? This was great! "Let's go check it out!" I said. "I'll bring my camera!"

"I will call Ken. He will come and get me, we will come and get you, and then all of us will go to Ono Beach to check things out. Good bye, Steve."

"Good bye, Mihn." I hung up, ran back upstairs, took a quick shower and got dressed. Then I snagged my camera, wrote GONE TO SEA A MONSTER. GET IT? next to STEVE on the blackboard, and went outside to wait in the driveway.

It wasn't long before I heard "Smoke on the Water" by Deep Purple, and just as Ken's Thunderbird came careening down Desdemona Street and up to the house, I wondered what Ms. Ellerath would have to say about that fact that the car was big and white and banged up a little. Just like Moby Dick. And I was a little worried about the fact that I was starting to think that way.

I got in the back seat – where Zombie was on his back and waiting for me to scratch his belly.

"*Chao buoi sang*," I said.

Mihn laughed. "Very good! Good morning to you, too."

I was relieved. The last time I tried a Vietnamese phrase out on Mihn, I ended up calling him "laxative ear" by mistake.

"*Chili con carne* to both of you." Ken said. "Let's drop the language lesson and go check out this terrifying sea monster."

72

"Yes," Mihn said. "This is ass exciting!"

Zombie purred. Or maybe he farted, it was hard to tell. Either way, it was an encouraging sound. And then we were off to Ono Beach to see the awful thing that would come to be known as Mister Fishback's Monster.

*"It was an experience that none of them would soon forget!"*

About halfway there, Ken cut the music. "I've got a great soundtrack idea for your movie," he said. "What's the title again, *Epic, Now?*"

"*Epoch Lost*," I said. "I thought you wanted me to use "Frankenstein" by The Edgar Winters Group." It was one on Ken's favorite songs, with lots of fuzzy bass.

"Right," Ken said. "It's perfect. But I think it would sound even cooler if you played it backwards."

"Backwards?" Mihn asked.

"It would be ominous," Ken said. "Trippy."

I thought for a second, trying to hear the song in my mind – backwards. "You might be right."

"Way trippy," Mihn said.

# Chapter Thirteen

Weird news travels fast. It seemed like half of Seaport was already down on Ono Beach, gathered in a gawking, murmuring, shutter clicking circle, just like after Kong took that big one-hundred-and-two-story header to the New York street back in 1933. Except this time, the subject of attention was a roughly sixty-foot-long, hopefully deceased, burrito-shaped lump of . . . something. At least that's what it looked like from where we stood in the parking lot up above the beach and through a shimmering, silvery, early morning haze.

"What is that thing?" Mihn asked.

"It's a monster." Ken clapped a leash on Zombie – who couldn't have been more thrilled to be going with us this time. "A sea monster."

"A dead sea monster?" Mihn asked.

"That's the best kind," Ken said.

"Let's get down there and check it out," I said, and the four of us started down the narrow, sandy trail to the beach – with Zombie leading the way – to get a better look.

*"Little did they know that their lives were about to change forever!"*

The gawkers were locals, mostly. You could tell by the wind-burned faces and the names of local fishing boats and volunteer fire departments on the back of their stained sweatshirts and faded wind breakers. There were a few tourists, too. They were the folks with the umbrellas. At first, I thought that maybe a whale had beached itself. That happens on the Oregon Coast from time to time. Nobody knows why they do it. But as I got closer to the big dead burrito, I could make out certain incongruous, non-cetacean, and very confusing details.

There was a long, pale row of suckers, as wide in diameter as my hand. Another row of smaller suckers. One giant flipper, with some of its finger bones exposed. Sharp, jutting teeth. Exposed and porous bone. Smooth skin in some places. Fur in others. Scales, too.

Mihn shook his head. "It's like that fable about the six blind men and the elephant."

"It was six men of Indostan," Ken said, reciting lines from the old poem, "to learning much inclined, who went to see the elephant, though each of them were blind."

Mihn was right. As we stood next to huge dead whatsit, it was hard to put all those pieces together into a mental whole that made any kind of sense, partly because half of the thing was shrouded in dirty, moldy rope netting, seaweed, and torn, ragged sections of what appeared to be old sail cloth. It was as if someone had cast a half-dozen of the world's largest sea creatures, named and unnamed, along with a ton or two of foreign, and possibly ancient, maritime debris, into a humongous blender, and then gave the entire mess a half crank, just enough to jumble it up. And above the entire, repulsive tangle, a lidless eye, suspended on a fleshy stalk of the kind you see on banana slugs, but big as a grapefruit, glared back at us – seemingly ashamed to be the subject of this sort of freebie freak show scrutiny and conjecture.

"It *is* a monster," I said. "No doubt about it. A for real monster."

Zombie sputtered and snapped and bared his teeth – but had the sense to keep a safe distance.

Not me. As I leaned closer to The Monster, I could smell the very bottom of the sea, far off places, and a long time ago.

*Where did it come from?*
*A mystery to be solved –*
*or best left alone?*

I'd been waiting my entire life to ask a specific question, THE classic sci-fi, monster movie question. And today was the day. I quickly, dramatically, removed my specs and turned to Ken. "What do you make of it?"

Ken was hip. First, he arched an eyebrow, and then he answered THE question with an answer worthy of the best sci-fi movie experts, like Robert Cornthwaite or Whit Bissel or even the great Frank C. Baxter. "I believe this is a creature heretofore unknown to science as we know it."

Whoa! I actually shivered as I realized that my best friends and I had all but stepped into one of the hokey movies I loved so much.

But Mihn didn't get it. "What are you two talking about?" I guess they didn't have late night monster movies in Vietnam. Too bad.

Two guys with hippie beards and pony tails and orange OSU sweatshirts were busy examining The Monster. I assumed they were marine biologists. The two were silent as they made measurements and took pictures and scraped tiny samples into glass vials.

I had to touch The Monster. Had to. This was a once in a lifetime, dream come true for me. And I'm sure that when I reached out to touch it, I looked just like one of those ape men in *2001: A Space Odyssey*. Life imitates art, I guess. Or is it the other way around?

But as I actually placed my palm flat against a smooth part of the thing, I thought for an instant that I'd been nailed by an icy sneaker wave, and at the same time I felt a very real, deep down fear, accompanied by a series of distinct and disturbing mental images – Steve-O-Scope, out of control. I saw snapping jaws and hungry eyes, surging at me from a dark, underwater place that suddenly turned from deep blue and green to bloody red. I heard the muffled howl of some wounded sea animal. It was a howl of intense pain. And fear.

I snatched my hand away, rubbed it, and put it back again. Nothing this time. I touched a rough spot, a furry place, and then I ran my finger along the edge of a long, cold tooth. Still nothing. I felt both disappointed and relieved at the same time.

"What's wrong?" Mihn asked.

"Nothing." I decided it was time to start shooting and immortalize this bizarre event. "I'll be right back."

Zombie stood up on his hind legs, whimpering and clawing the air as if telling me to be careful.

Of course, the big, for real movie studios have swinging cranes and wheeled dollies. I didn't even have a zoom lens. But I was pretty good at moving in and out of live action by taking slow, shuffling steps so that I wouldn't stumble and then mess up the shot. I started at the edge of the crowd.

And . . . action! My injured eye ached as I squinted into the viewfinder. I made quiet swooshing sounds as made my way through and around folks, always including just a glimpse of The Monster in the background. I wasn't rigged for sound, but I could hear the various opinions and verdicts.

"Looks like a whale."

"Right whale. Or parts of one, anyways."

"Last time I checked, whales didn't have tentacles."

"Or brown fur."

Swoosh, whoosh. I panned from one yapping face to another as I moved closer to the star of this show, riffing with the camera like a jazz musician with a saxophone.

"Walruses don't grow that big."

"Thing musta been caught in a Nipponese drift net."

And then, right on cue, Richard Trammell, a senior member of the Siletz Tribe and reputed to be the oldest living human in Seaport, if not the entire Oregon Coast, stepped out of the gawkers and self-appointed experts and right into the center of my shot. His face was lined and red and he had a white beard. He wore a faded Mexican *sarape*, and a knit cap like the one Jack Nicholson wore in *One Flew Over the Cuckoo's Nest*.

Mister Trammell had been, at different times in his life, a bare knuckle fighter, a blimp captain, searching the Oregon Coast for Japanese subs, and an oyster pirate. Whatever that is. Hard work and age had stooped him a little, and he needed two canes, each carved of gnarled and varnished driftwood, to get around these days.

His prophet's beard parting in the wind, the old man limped up to The Monster. I followed him, hoping he would touch it and then have the same kind of bizarre, out of body experience I'd just had. Everybody else, including other old timers, kept quiet, waiting for a proclamation of some sort.

Mister Trammell didn't actually touch The Monster, but when he poked at it with one of his canes, the thing shifted, moved, and a deep, low groan came from somewhere inside. Men shouted. A girl screamed. I was startled, but like a trooper, I held the camera rock still.

Mister Trammell didn't move, either. He stood fast, eyes narrowed, ready to go to blows with The Monster if need be. But then it seemed to settle, quiet down, go back to sleep. I kept the camera steady, because I knew, I just *knew*, that Mister Trammell was about to say something important, dramatic.

He did not disappoint.

"My Indian ancestors warned of this," he said. "This is a foretelling, a warning, from both Mother Earth, and the deep green sea of our fisherman fathers. We are all arrogant and disrespectful children, we've taken much more than we've given back, and we will be punished!"

Nobody said anything. Some folks nodded in agreement.

Then Mister Trammell turned to the crowd, held up one of his canes as if it was Moses' staff, and said, "Mark my words, and mark them well. One day soon, the bitter blood of judgment will rain down out of a clear sky to defile us, and mark us all as guilty!"

A collective shiver washed over the crowd. Murmurs. Whispers.

Blood? I wondered. Clear sky? I kept rolling.

Mister Trammell tapped one of the OSU guys with a cane. "So what do you college boys think?"

The OSU guy shrugged. "I'm not sure. Maybe it's several animals, all thrown together, like a multispecies car wreck."

The second OSU guy pulled aside a curtain of

dirty, shaggy seaweed, revealing a very deep, very mean-looking gash, maybe three feet by four feet. "This appears to be an injury."

"What could have caused that?" Mister Trammell asked.

"A propeller, maybe," the second OSU guy said. "A big one. Maybe that's what killed it."

I moved in close to the injury, or scar, or whatever it was, and back out again. Then I panned past Mister Trammell, and across the staring, open mouth crowd.

Cut! I checked the footage gauge on my camera. I had a hundred feet of film left.

I found Ken, Mihn and Zombie. "I've got a monster," I said, "an angry mob, some ancient Indian superstition, and a couple of scientists. I'm going to build a flick around this!"

"Coming soon to a theater near you," Ken said, in his Orson the Tiger, showman voice. "A humble biology teacher discovers the dead remains of a freakish creature. What is this thing, this nightmare beast from the ocean's deepest region? Where did it come from? The world holds its collective breath! Be sure to see . . ." He turned to me. "Any ideas for a title?"

I was ready. "*Mister Fishback's Monster*!"

Mihn laughed and clapped and quoted Jimmy Walker, a TV character that was very popular at the time: "Dyn-O-Mite!"

"Right on," Ken said. "Give me five!"

As Ken and Mihn started in on what they believed to be a very righteous, soul-brother handshake, I noticed Julie Smith, blond hair blowing across her curious expression and neck brace partially concealed by the hood of her sweatshirt, standing arm-in-arm with her big and scary logger dad, just a few yards away.

I cranked up the film speed. (That's how slow motion works. The faster the film speed, the smaller the difference between one frame and the next, and the slower the resulting action.) Then I rubbed the camera lens with my index finger so that the shot would be just a little blurry. Soft focus, they call it.

Action! Holding the camera about waist-high, aiming the lens at Julie, and hoping for a well-framed, medium close up, I ran off a few feet of film.

Cut! Now I had a pretty girl for my monster flick. Perfect.

A Coast Guard helicopter swooped in, and hovered above us. Zombie ran up Ken's leg and then under his letterman jacket. I grabbed a quick shot of the chopper.

"For realism, right?" Ken asked.

"You got it," I said. "Realism."

"Of course," Ken said, "if the three of us are characters in this monster movie of yours, Mihn will have to get killed."

"That is not fair!" Mihn looked hurt. "Why me?"

"No offense," Ken said. "You're a racial minority. Movies have rules, right, Steve?"

"Don't worry, Mihn," I said. "If I have to kill you off, I'll give you a spectacular death."

"Thank you." Mihn seemed genuinely grateful.

By this time, I was almost out of film. "I need a master shot," I said. A master shot is a camera angle that takes in a large area. It's like the opposite of a close up. Movie directors use master shots to give the audience an introduction, an overview to a scene before going in for closer shots. "Be right back."

"Roger that," Ken said. "We'll be right here."

"Yes," Mihn said. "Roger."

81

I started back up the trail, to higher ground. Along the way, I wiped the camera lens clean with my shirt and set the film speed back to normal. Up in the parking lot, the mist was nearly gone. I lined up a nice master shot of Ono beach, the crowd, and The Monster – with Ken's white Thunderbird in the slightly blurry foreground. Arty, huh?

Action! This will be a great opener, I thought, but then Ronny Behr's smiling, broken-nosed face suddenly filled my viewfinder.

"That's a nice camera," he said. "Give it to me!"

Cut! I shrugged and shook my head, and before I could say or do anything, a giant hand with three clawed fingers grabbed Ronny by the right foot, and then hoisted him, upside down, into the air. My long gone Nixon-lookin' Cyclops, the very one Ronny had smashed in the eighth grade, was repaired, alive, pissed off, and about twenty-five feet high.

*"The great titan had returned to exact his terrible vengeance!"*

The mythical beast rocked back a bit, Harryhausen-style, worked its lower jaw from side to side, snarled with a voice that sounded like a logging truck engine-braking, and hungrily studied Ronny with that one squinty, twitching, ravenous eye. But before I could order my Tricky Dick Cyclops not to eat Ronny, and to maybe just dunk him in the ocean a few times, I felt a deep pain in my right shoulder.

The Nixon Cyclops went away, and Ronny punched me again. "I said give me that camera!"

I held my camera's close to my body, and started for Ken's T-Bird so that I could jump inside, and lock all the doors. But before I could break into a run and maybe have a chance of getting away, Ronny started punching me in the shoulder, knuckle punching me, over and over. It hurt. A lot. But I hung on to that camera with both hands. I knew that Ronny was stronger than me, and that if I let go with one hand, to either punch back or push Ronny away, he would grab the camera, and that I would never see it again.

"Give it!" Frothy spit came out of Ronny's mouth. We started playing tug of war with my camera.

"No!" I didn't care how much it hurt, I was not about to let go of that camera, not about to surrender a single frame of the film I'd shot. "No way!"

Ronny laughed and punched me even harder. Just as I was about to yell for help, another hand – three of its fingers held together with ketchup-streaked first aid tape – grabbed Ronny Behr's wrist and squeezed. Hard.

"Leave my buddy alone!" Ken said.

Ronny cursed in pain and started dancing around, and for a second I thought Ken would actually crush Ronny's wrist. I fully expected to hear joints popping and bones breaking. My shoulder burned, and I couldn't move my elbow or my fingers much. But I was free. More importantly, so was my camera, and the film inside.

Mihn held Zombie's leash. "Easy, Ken."

Zombie hissed and slobbered and bobbed his bald, scarred head up and down.

Ken released Ronny. Then he slugged Ronny right in the chest. Ronny made a sound like Mister Fishback's Monster had made when Mister Trammell poked it with his cane, just not as loud. Then, with all the wind knocked out of him, Ronny fell backward onto the sandy blacktop, gasping for air.

Ken stood over Ronny like Kong standing over a just-thrashed Tyrannosaurus. He kicked at Ronny. "Stop picking on my buddy!"

Ronny managed a breath or two. And when he opened his mouth to answer, blood drooled out. When he felt the blood running down his chin, he let out a roar.

Zombie ran at Ronny, snarling and spitting – and then choking when he ran out of leash.

"Looks like you bit your tongue, there, sport." I thought Ken actually felt sorry for Ronny. He winced. "You're going to need stitches."

Ronny said something through a mouthful of blood, but we couldn't understand him. He got up, flipped me the missing finger bird, and then stomped off.

"You leave my friend alone!" Ken didn't chase after Ronny. "I don't want to get blood on my hundred and fifty-dollar jacket, that's all!"

"Thanks, Ken." Once again, I was grateful for Ken's intervention, and just like before, I was also ashamed. "I'm such a wuss."

Ken squeezed his hurt-all-over-again fingers, and smiled at me. "Give yourself some credit. You held on to your camera. You protected your movie. I admire you for that."

"Maybe you're right." I felt a little better. Just a little. "Man, my shoulder hurts!"

"It'll hurt even more tomorrow," Ken said. "That's rock and roll, my friend. No pain, no gain."

"No pain," I said, offering an alternative to the old saying, "fine with me."

"I do not think we have heard the last from Ronny ass Behr," Mihn said.

"I think you are right," Ken said.

I knew it, too.

As we stood there in the parking lot, the wind picked up just a little, and a dank, rotten smell blew up from the beach.

"Pew," Ken said.

*"It was an ominous omen of the olfactory awfulness to come!"*

"What was that talk about blood raining down out of a clear sky?" Mihn asked.

"Beats me," I said. "It sounded like something out of the Old Testament."

"These are the days of plagues and monsters," Ken said, "And monsters give us meaning."

"Meaning?" That sounded so cool. "How?"

Ken patted his letterman jacket, searching for a pepperoni stick, but I guess he was out. "Have you ever seen those maps of the Old World, the ones with the corny sea serpents and dragons swimming around in the ocean?" This was the analytic, chess club, opera singing side of Ken, not the rock and roll, wrestler side that we had seen a few minutes before when he slugged Ronny in the chest and knocked him down. "Only a few sailors were brave enough to accept the challenge, courageous enough to set sail on a sea of monsters. Without big-bellied monsters, there would be no heroes."

"You sound like Ms. Ellerath," I said.

"After the Communists took Saigon in 1975," Mihn said, "my family set sail on a sea of monsters, too."

I wasn't sure what Mihn was talking about. But I guess Ken knew about the Vietnam War and what had happened after the war ended. He leaned to one side so that his elbow touched Mihn's shoulder. "I'm glad you guys made it out, man."

"Me, too," I said.

"Me, too," Mihn said.

Zombie barked in agreement, and his eyes blinked

independently of each other. Poor Zomb.

We stayed like that for several minutes, three good friends and the world's ugliest ferret. Down on the beach, the crowd had grown even larger. Dark clouds were moving in over the sea. More rain was on the way.

*"Would the approaching storm bring another abyssal monstrosity?"*

"Let's roll." The Thunderbird rocked to the left as Ken got in. "We have a mystery to solve."

"And a monster flick to shoot." I climbed into the back seat. If my shoulder was going to hurt even worse tomorrow morning, I was going to be in rough shape.

"Sounds like a very strange Hardy Boys story." Mihn handed me Zombie's leash, and took shotgun. Zombie ran up under my shirt and immediately buried his cold, wet face in my arm pit.

Goggles in place, Ken started the T-Bird. "Let's go see what Crazy Annie knows about sea monsters."

"Crazy?" Mihn had never met the woman.

"She's not crazy," I said. "Not really."

"Her brain got fried in the sixties," Ken said.

"We don't know that for sure," I said.

Mihn didn't like the sound of fried brains. "Crazy Annie is a dope fiend?"

"Annie knows things about the Oregon Coast that nobody else knows." Ken put the Thunderbird into first gear. "But if she offers you a brownie, whatever you do, don't eat it. Not if you want to stay sane."

Mihn stared out the windshield and didn't say a word, but I saw his Adam's apple move up and down.

# Chapter Fourteen

Crazy Annie's was just a few miles up the Coast Highway. Her funky old shop, perched on a cliff above a rocky inlet, looked like a cheap matte painting from a Roger Corman movie: Sagging, moss-covered roof. Crooked smokestack. The silhouette of a cat in the front window. A single, windblown pine tree.

*"It was a place where time and logic had been all but forgotten!"*

Annie sold old books and all kinds of odd, obscure things that you couldn't find anywhere else. Persian rugs. Incense. Tribal masks. Scrimshawed whale teeth. Her homemade brownies were also popular for some highly suspicious and allegedly illegal reason. But you couldn't buy bait there.

Annie knew everything there was to know about coastal history, geography, weather conditions, whale migration patterns. And, we hoped, washed up monsters from the deep.

Ken pulled up the Thunderbird next to that lonely pine tree. For some reason, Zombie ran under the car seat and refused to come out.

"Are you sure this is a good-ass idea?" Mihn asked.

"Absolutely," Ken said.

The clouds were darker than a few minutes before. The wind was almost cold, now. It was like a low-budget, cinematic foreshadowing of some impending discovery or event, and I loved it.

As we entered the shop, I smelled incense, old

paper and binding glue – and fresh-baked fudge.

I heard Ken's stomach growl. "Easy big fella," I said.

"I'm OK," Ken said.

"What is that?" Mihn pointed to a wooden chest with a glass case on top of it, just inside the doorway. Inside the case was a twisted, mummified figure, about eight inches long, suspended in tattered fish netting. It had piranha teeth, clutching fingers, a scaly, fish-type body tail. And a tiny gold earring. "It looks like a bald monkey with fins."

"It's a genuine Burmese mermaid," Ken said.

"Mermaid?" Mihn read from a paper label inside the case. "This bizarre creature was captured in the waters off Rangoon in 1944. Alive when caught, the animal emitted high, thin howling sounds, as if calling to others of its kind, and died within an hour. According to traditional folklore, creatures such as this were possessed of great wisdom."

Ken and I had seen the Burmese Mermaid at least a dozen times before. I was about ninety percent it was a sideshow fake, but it still gave me chills. The eyes didn't look wild or ferocious, just weary and lost.

Ken: "Maybe it knows."

Mihn: "Knows what?"

Me: "Maybe the Burmese Mermaid can tell us about The Monster." I put my hands on my knees, bent over the odd exhibit, and whispered, "What is that dead thing on Ono Beach? Where did it come from?" My breath fogged the glass a little. "Why was Moby Dick white?"

We waited for an answer. And we all jumped at the sound of dry, high-pitched laughter, coming from the other side of the shop, where Crazy Annie sat behind an old sea captain's desk, dressed all in black.

The high shelf behind her was packed with books and sea shells and weathered nautical instruments.

Annie had a wrinkled face, white hair, gray eyes, and looked for all the world like one of those fortune teller robots with gears and levers inside it. I wanted to steal a quick shot of the old bat, but I wasn't sure how she might react. I didn't think there was enough light, anyway.

When Crazy Annie raised a skeletal hand and pointed at me, I could almost hear the whir and click of tiny mechanical parts. "You saw it," she said. "This morning. You saw the thing, didn't you?"

"Yes, ma'am," I said. "We all did."

"How did she know that?" Mihn whispered.

"She's like that," Ken whispered back.

I stepped up to the desk. "We were wondering if you could tell us what it might be."

When Annie stood up she was only slightly taller than when she'd been sitting. "Of course, whales have beached themselves on our beaches many times." Annie came out from behind her desk. Her long black dress touched the floor so you couldn't see her feet.

"We're pretty sure it isn't a whale," I said.

"Pretty sure," Ken said.

Mihn kept quiet.

"Let me show you something." Annie whirled and glided across the floor as if on wheels. We followed in descending order of height: Me, Ken, and then Mihn, to an adjoining room that looked like a retired pirate's office. There were aboriginal clubs and knives on the walls. Charts. A brass telescope on a tripod, pointing through French windows and down to the gray sea. And an oil painting, resting on a brass easel. "Take a look," Annie said. "Take a good look."

Ken and Mihn and I tilted out heads at the same

angle and concentrated on the painting. The image swirled with dark blues and greens and a lot of black. It was darkest at the center, and grew lighter toward the edges. It was like one of those abstract paintings that only artists and junior college art teachers and people on PBS can explain.

*"It was a disturbing image, both repulsive and compelling!"*

"What is that?" Ken asked. "I can't tell."

Mihn nudged me. "It's like that painting in *Moby Dick*," he whispered. "Ishmael could not figure it out for a long time, but then he realized that it was a picture of a giant whale, leaping up out of the water, and impaling itself on the mast of a ship. It freaked his ass out."

On cue, the room turned dark. Rain hissed on the French windows.

"I see an eye," Ken said. "Yep, an eye." He pointed. Sure enough, a single angry eye, rimmed in yellow and gold, stared out at us. And then the rest of the image fell into place: A long, serpentine neck. Teeth. Clawed flippers.

"That's a Plesiosaurus," I said.

*"It was the fanged, flippered terror of prehistoric seas!"*

Annie chuckled. "It was sighted at the mouth of the Columbia River in 1934."

"1934?" I asked. "Plesiosaurs lived during the Jurassic Period, one hundred million years ago. I don't get it."

"The first mate on the Columbia River Lightship described the beast as being at least forty feet in length with a long neck and an evil, snake head." Annie could've narrated trailers. "An identical beast was sighted in 1937, swimming at the end of Old Jetty."

"Old Jetty," I said. "Just a few miles down the road. Dad and I went crabbing there just the other day."

"The dead animal we saw this morning had fur," Mihn said.

"So did Old Hairy," Annie said. "That's what the locals called the dead beastie that washed up north of here in 1950. They also said it had nine tails. Scientists were unable to identify it."

"Nine tails?" Ken asked. "Weird!"

"Oregon has a long history of monsters," Annie said. "Members of the Siletz tribe warned Lewis and Clark about a tentacled demon living at the bottom of Devil's Lake back in 1805."

I made myself turn away from Annie's creepy monster painting so that I wouldn't have dreams about it later.

Annie laughed just a little too loud and a little too long. "You didn't think Big Foot was Oregon's only monster, did you?" She laughed even louder and floated her way out of the room.

Pale sunlight shone through the French windows. The rain let up and turned to blowing mist.

By now, Mihn was more than a little freaked. "Who is this Big Foot?" he asked. "Is he a local monster? Does he step on people, or something?"

"I'll fill you in later," Ken said. "I know a good Big Foot story. Let's cruise."

On our way out, we thanked Annie for her time and knowledge.

"Would you boys like some brownies?" she asked, inner mechanisms spinning and chattering along. "They're free."

At that, Mihn ran out of the place.

"No thank you." I didn't want to get hooked on drugs, shanghaied, and then wake up in the middle of some Singapore slave auction.

But I could see that Ken was tempted to take Annie up on her offer. "Fudge brownies?"

Annie held up a silver tray, stacked with thick brown squares. "Help yourself."

"We've got to get going." I tugged on the sleeve of Ken's letterman jacket. Ken whimpered a little, but it was for his own good.

But before we left, I had to ask Annie about another mysterious sea beast. "Have you ever read *Moby Dick* by Herman Melville?"

"Moby Dick?" The servos in Annie's skull buzzed and spun and created a smile. "Of course."

"Why is the whale white? It's for school."

Crazy Annie's teeth clicked as she spoke. "Maybe the white whale is a symbol for all the evil done by the Caucasian race, all over the world. Conquest. War. Slavery."

"That's pretty deep." Would Ms. Ellerath buy that answer? Probably. I led Ken past the Burmese mermaid and out the door.

Mihn was waiting for us outside. "Did you eat the brownies? Are you two high on dope?"

"Negatory." I looked at Ken. "But that was a close one."

Ken squeezed into the front seat of his T-Bird. "Brownies are my weakness. No doubt about it."

Mihn laughed as he held the seat for me. "So are other people's French fries, ass wheel."

I hopped in back. Zombie came out of hiding, ran up my leg and arm and up to the top of my aching shoulder. Then he started licking my face. His tongue was hot.

Ken cranked the engine, revved it a little. "Where to? What next?"

There was a monster in town. A real monster. I

92

wanted to take in as much of this B-movie experience as I possibly could. "I don't know about you two, but I want to camp out on Ono Beach tonight, just in case something happens."

"What could happen?" Mihn asked.

"Maybe that thing will wake up," Ken said. "Maybe it will come back to life and . . !"

I didn't hear the rest because Zombie sneezed right in my ear.

"I would hate to miss that," Mihn said.

"Neither would I," Ken said. "Let's grab our sleeping bags, some grub, a few chicks, and then spend the night on the beach with a dead monster."

"Should be easy," I said. "Except for the chicks, that is."

"Of course, I'm spoken for." Ken turned to Mihn with a grin. "I have a beautiful Vietnamese girlfriend."

Mihn gave Ken the middle finger, and you could tell he hadn't had much practice.

Ken giggled, put the Bird in reverse, and backed up to the service road. He ejected a cassette tape and, without looking, replaced it with another. The car was suddenly filled with "Mama Mia," a song by the Swedish group, ABBA.

I was shocked. "Since when do you listen to ABBA?

"Gahh!" Ken smashed the eject button with a caveman finger, pulled the cassette out of the dashboard, and tossed it out the window. "That is not my tape! That is not my tape! I hate ABBA!"

Zombie trembled.

I checked Ken's face in the rear view mirror. He didn't look angry. He looked like he'd just been caught. Was Ken a secret ABBA fan?

"I like ABBA," Mihn said. "What is your big ass

deal?"

Ken put on his goggles and turned to Mihn with a fuzzy scowl. "ABBA ain't rock and roll!" He grabbed another cassette, checked the label this time, jammed it into the tape player, and cranked up the volume. Then we were off, headed back to Seaport – and cruising to the hard beat of Iron Butterfly.

Ten minutes later, Ken and Mihn dropped me off in front of our house on Desdemona Street. "We'll be back around six," Ken said.

"Right on," I said. "See ya then."

Mihn waved as the T-Bird pulled a U-ey and then departed the scene. Zombie bug-eyed me from the back seat.

I went inside, upstairs, and put my hand on Stephanie's door. "You wouldn't believe it!" I said. "There's a monster on Ono Beach! It's a big dead thing with teeth and scales and even some fur. I shot some film of it. Then Ronny slugged me in the shoulder a bunch of times and tried to steal my camera from me! Ken saved the day." I took a breath. "We went to see Crazy Annie, and she said there have been a lot of monsters in Oregon."

No reply.

"We're going to camp out on the beach tonight. Yeah, it might rain, but that's OK."

Nothing. All of a sudden, I felt brave enough to go inside. But then I chickened out again.

"I wish you could come with us, Steph." I went down the hall to my room. I took my camera into the closet, and closed the door behind me. In total darkness and working by feel, I removed the Brachiosaurus/Ono Beach film from the old camera, put it in a metal film can, and then tucked that film can safely away in the pocket of my winter parka. I had worked too hard to lose my film to either sunlight or Ma's snooping. Then I loaded a fresh roll.

# Chapter Fifteen
## Dusk

"It was the summer of 1924. Twilight in the cool shadow of Mount Saint Helens. An old prospector kneeled at the edge of the Lewis River. It had been a long, tiring day, panning for gold. As the man dipped his canteen into the clear water one last time, he listened to the sounds of wild birds and bugs, and the wind, high in the conifers, and he looked forward to dinner with the three other prospectors in their log cabin, and then a good night's sleep. But then, just as sudden as the snap of a sheet . . ." Ken paused for dramatic effect.

We had assembled a small driftwood hideout, complete with a tarp roof in case it rained, and a campfire, above the high water line and just up the beach from Mister Fishback's Monster.

"Silence," Ken whispered.

"Silence." Mihn whispered, too.

I rubbed my sore shoulder but didn't say anything. This was Ken's show. His flick.

"And when the prospector looked up," Ken said, "he saw something on the other side of the river, something the likes of which he had never seen before."

Mihn swallowed. "What did he see? An Indian? A ghost? An Indian ghost? Dracula?"

"None of the above." Ken leaned toward the fire, and the flickering firelight created eerie shadows on his unshaven face. "He saw what he thought might be an ape, half-standing, half-hunched over, hairy arms hanging down, and staring right at him."

"Are there apes in Oregon?" Mihn asked.

"Not outside the Portland Zoo," Ken said. "The prospector ran back to the cabin. He locked the door and blew out the lantern and told the other prospectors about what he had seen. They all hid their bags of gold under a board in the floor. Then they grabbed their rifles and their ammo. The first prospector went to the window, but when he looked outside, back across the river, the creature was gone."

"Gone," Mihn said. "Disappeared back into the woods." It was like Ken and Mihn were both telling the same story.

"The others accused the first prospector of lying," Ken said. "An hour or so later, the four prospectors ate dinner and went to bed and they were all sleeping soundly when . . ." Ken paused again. "Wham! Bam! Rocks came crashing down on their cabin!"

"Rocks!"

"Huge river rocks, bigger than any man could even carry, let alone throw through the air. They battered the cabin roof and walls and the prospectors thought the little building would be crushed!"

"Crushed!"

"Smashed to splinters. The first prospector opened a window and fired his rifle into the dark, even though he couldn't see anything, over and over. When he ran out of ammo, one of the other men tossed him a fresh rifle." Ken made the sound of a rifle cocking and then firing. "He didn't know if he hit anything or not, but suddenly the rocks stopped coming down, and the prospectors heard the sounds of chirping crickets and hooting owls. The creatures were gone. But the next morning, when the prospectors felt safe enough to emerge from their cabin, they found dozens of huge, bare footprints. The smallest ones were eighteen inches long."

"That is amazing!"

"And then as the prospectors stood there in awed silence, they heard a sound echo from the very deepest part of the forest. It was an eerie sound. It was the howl of Big Foot."

"Big Foot?" Mihn asked. "What did it sound like?"

"It was a wild, haunting sound, and it hung in the air, just like this."

I thought for sure that Ken was going to rise up on one cheek and then squeeze off a long, loud fart. But instead of cranking one out, Ken let out a low, bass note from somewhere deep in his diaphragm and held it for a long time. Then he brought the howl up and out and sent it off into the twilight.

"Creepy," Mihn said. Then he shivered. "If I was out in the woods and heard that sound, I would not know whether to defecate or go blind."

"And it actually happened," Ken said.

The ocean hissed and roared. The waves boomed when they broke on the shore. The sun went down, and then we couldn't see The Monster anymore. Our campfire flickered and snapped.

"I wonder what that dead thing actually is," I said.

"Don't wonder too much," Ken said. "There's probably some very logical, very scientific, very disappointing explanation for it."

"Probably," I said. "I hate those movies where the big scary monster turns out to be either swamp gas, or a hoax."

"Then again," Ken said, "maybe Annie was right about Oregon monsters."

"I hope so." I wanted to believe that there were

real monsters out there – as long as they didn't hurt anybody.

"I have a scary ass story of my own to tell you," Mihn said. "And there are monsters in it. Real scary monsters."

Ken and I settled back. "Go ahead," Ken said.

Mihn stared into the fire. "People said the Communists could read children's minds, and that they knew our anti-Communist thoughts. People said the Communists would kill all of our elders, all of our teachers, and even anyone that wore glasses.

My father told them not to panic, but at the same time he began to sell his fishing equipment, and he exchanged much of our money for gold since our Vietnam money would be worthless in other countries. He also studied maps, and talked to other fishermen about the open sea. My father wanted to be ready if the worst happened, but he did not want anyone else to know.

Then a day came when relatives from Saigon came to our town, carrying everything they owned, and they told us about terrible torture and execution. My country was dead, and a new one had taken its place, so we decided that it was time to leave.

There were ten of us – two families – on my father's boat the night we left Vietnam. I was shaking. My mother cried. Mai cried, too, but she tried to hide her tears from the kids.

When the sun came up, we were surrounded on all sides by smooth blue water. We were many miles from home. My father looked brave as he steered our boat and watched the water for other boats. The kids were scared because they had never been so far from home, so I read to them from *The Old Man and the Sea*, by Mister Ernest Hemingway, even though they didn't understand English.

Late on the second night, Thai pirates found our boat. They laughed and smiled with silver and gold teeth, and they snapped and barked like wild dogs, and they ordered us to give them all our food and money. The pirates might have been beautiful innocent babies once, but I could see they did not have souls any more. They were monsters, now.

I took Mai down into the hold of the boat, because I didn't want the pirates to see her, but there was no place to hide. I did not know what else to do, so I took out a straight razor."

Ken started to say something, maybe ask why, but he stopped.

"Mai cried. I put my hand over her mouth. I slapped her face. Then I cut her hair. Later, when the pirates found Mai, they left her alone because they thought she was a boy. They took two of the other girls, though. They were both very young. Very young. Please do not ask me about what the pirates did to them. It was awful. It was ass, ass awful."

That was the end of Mihn's monster story.

We stayed up a little longer, talked, and made some popcorn. Mihn had never seen Jiffy Pop before, and he got a big kick out of it. There were a few other campfires up and down Ono Beach. Somewhere, someone blew a harmonica. When the air got a little too chilly, we got into our sleeping bags. The talking died down. I think Mihn was the first one to fall asleep.

I thought about Mihn's story, and how he seemed so happy and positive despite all that had happened in his life. How did he deal with it? Did he slip off into a fantasy world, too?

Ken called my name in a loud whisper.

batka

"What is it?" I asked.

A quieter whisper this time. "I'm going to marry Mai, you know."

"OK." It had been an amazing day of best friends and bullies, monsters and metaphors. Pam Grier and I decided that it would be bad manners for us to rub noses tonight, so we just spooned and listened to the ocean until we fell asleep.

Sometime during the night, Pam woke me up. "I have to pee. Come with me."

"Where are you going?" I asked.

"To the water. Come with me."

"I don't have to go," I said. "Besides, it's chilly."

"C'mon, candy ass!" Hazy moonlight sparkled in Pam's Afro like electricity. "What kind of man lets a defenseless female walk on the beach at night?"

"You? Defenseless?"

Pam Grier wasn't in the habit of taking no for an answer, but I was her boyfriend, her main man, so I had the last say. And as she ran down to the surf she must've known that I was watching – and that I was still watching when she pulled off her blue jean cutoffs, and walked out into the water until she was waist deep. Then she turned and waved.

I waved back. As Pam peed, I couldn't help but wonder if there was another sea monster out there – or maybe a Sharkasaurus Rex – and that I should have accompanied her. But just as a huge grill of moon-gleaming teeth came chattering up out of the surf behind her, Pam finished up and came running back to me.

"Damn, that water's cold!" she said, and got back into the spoon.

"It's a tad warmer than it was a few minutes ago," I said – out loud apparently, because Ken started in

**101**

his sleep and sat up.

"What was that?" He rolled over. "Did The Monster wake up? Did it eat somebody?"

"No," I said, only mildly upset that Ken had just ruined a perfectly good nose rubbing opportunity. "Go back to sleep."

# Chapter Sixteen

## Tuesday Morning

When I woke up, the sun was still on the other side of the Summit. The eastern sky was pink and orange – with no sign of Mister Trammell's blood storm.

The tide was way out, and the ocean was dark blue-green-gray behind layers of salty, white, hissing fog, and there were bright white and yellow dots out on horizon – tuna trawlers. The chilly air smelled of dead seaweed and kelp and wood smoke. Our fire had gone out in the night. Mister Fishback's Monster was just a charcoal smudge, now.

This was the haiku-poetic, Monet-impressionistic, watercolor painting Oregon Coast that I loved so much.

*The fog conceals truth.*
*Fog can also reveal truth.*
*Fog knows the difference.*

My shoulder was stiff and deep-muscle sore, but I felt kinda good about the pain. I had earned it, after all, protecting my flick from being stolen. My eye felt a lot better.

Mihn crawled out his sleeping bag, shivering a little. "I need to urinate."

"Me, too." The sound of ocean waves can really make you want to go.

Mihn stood. "Where are the bathrooms?"

I looked around. There was a thick driftwood log just a few yards away. "Follow me."

Mihn and I went around to the leeward side of the log, assumed an appropriate interval between us, and peed into the sand.

"I admire you for what you did to save your sister." I wished I could've saved Stephanie somehow.

"I had to do it." And then Mihn said something that kind of freaked me out. It was like he knew what I was thinking. "There was nothing you could have done." He was talking about Stephanie's death.

Ken joined us, unzipped, and started whizzing away. "Are we not men?"

"We are men," Mihn said. "We are three men urinating in public."

What would Ms. Ellerath have to say about three good friends, three guys, standing together and peeing in public? I put that question right out of my head.

I finished first, then Ken. For a smaller guy, Mihn had an enormous bladder capacity. We washed our hands by rubbing them in the dry sand. Then we walked down to the water, rolled our pant legs up to our knees, waded out, and splashed sea water on our faces and in our hair and swished our mouths out with it.

"Just like Lewis and Clark," Mihn said.

"What if Hermann Melville had set *Moby Dick* on the West Coast instead of the East Coast?" I asked. "How would the story be different?"

"More rain," Mihn said. "More trees, and more Indians."

"The Makah tribe used to chase whales in canoes and throw harpoon in 'em," Ken said. "It's illegal, now, of course."

"That would be an interesting book," Mihn said.

"Or a cool movie," I said.

After cleaning up, we went back to our sleeping bags, ate cold blueberry Pop-Tarts for breakfast, and let our feet dry. Ken went back to sleep. Mihn had actually brought *Moby Dick* with him, and read from it. I sat back, looked up at the brightening sky, and wondered what would be the next scene in our real life monster movie. It wasn't long before I found out.

Mihn was the first to notice. "Something's going on."

I could see The Monster more clearly now – surrounded by people again. But this time, things were different. Everyone seemed to be moving, excited about something. There were more people, running down the trail to the beach. "What's the deal?" Then I noticed the Channel Two News van, up in the parking lot.

Ken sat up. "Did it wake up, or something? Did it eat somebody?"

"Let's go find out," I said.

We put on our socks and shoes, rolled up our sleeping bags, and strapped them to Ken's back. My camera was wound up and ready for action.

"Maybe we will be on TV," Mihn said.

When we got close to The Monster, we saw that there was at least one thing that was different about it: Someone had spray painted CLASS OF 1979 on one of the smoother parts. I grabbed a quick shot.

"Good morning, Oregon!" Chip Boost, a reporter for Channel Two, suddenly appeared, spouting his signature phrase. Two people clapped. Maybe three. Chip's hair looked like it was a varnished woodcarving, and his smile was so bright and perfectly aligned as to be distracting. He wore a yellow Channel Two windbreaker, and held a Styrofoam cup of

105

coffee. "So, this your sea monster?"

People murmured in the affirmative.

"Disgusting." Then Chip scanned the crowd. "Where is our professor?"

A man, tall, thin, wearing a sea captain's beard and a gray Oz High School sweatshirt, stepped up. "I'm not a professor," the man said. "I'm actually a high school biology teacher."

It was Mister Fishback!

Chip and Mister F. shook hands. "And you were the one that found this monster?" Chip took a sip of coffee.

"I don't know if I'd call it a monster." You could tell that Mister Fishback was having a blast. "But yes, I almost ran into the thing. I was walking along, minding my own business . . ."

"Save it for when we're rolling, Professor."

"Right."

The small TV crew took command of the scene, positioning Chip and Mister Fishback so that the good folks at home would see the two of them in the foreground of the shot, the still growing crowd right behind them, and then The Monster looming in the hazy background. A thin woman gave Chip's hair a quick touch up.

The Channel Two camera guy, a hippy-lookin' dude with a beard and granny glasses, hoisted an expensive-looking sixteen millimeter camera onto his shoulder and lined up the shot.

"Cool rig," I said.

But Camera Guy ignored me.

The sun had breached the Summit by now. The ocean mist had thinned. My friends and I stood together. As usual, Ken stood behind us. "I've never been on TV before," he said.

106

"Neither have I," Mihn said.

Neither had I.

"Will this be live?" Ken asked.

"I don't think so," I said. "I don't see any video cameras or cables or anything." And then two thoughts came to me. First, was Ronny Behr somewhere in the crowd of people, waiting to pants me on film? Second, where was Julie Smith and her tiny nose? It would be so cool if she was a part of all this.

"Are you ready, Professor?" Chip handed his coffee to the hair lady.

"Ready as I'll ever be," Mister Fishback said.

"Let's get this creep show on the road." Chip assumed an authoritative posture, stared into the camera, and waited. "This is a job for Ravenswort."

Camera Guy started rolling. "In three, two, one."

Chip was on. "It's a story right out of a science fiction movie," he said. "A dead creature of unknown origin, a monster, has washed ashore here in the sleepy coastal town of Seaport, causing quite a stir among the local folks. The man that actually found the thing, Professor Fishback, is here with us." Chip turned to Mister F. "Professor, from what I understand, you discovered this horrifying monster while jogging this morning. Is that correct?"

"That's right, Chip," Mister Fishback said, a little too loudly. "You see, I dropped a diving helmet on my right foot not long ago, so I haven't been able to go running in the morning. Well, I was feeling pretty OK today, and decided to make a quick jog . . ."

Chip interrupted. "And that's when you found the monster?"

"That's right. In fact, I almost ran right into the *dahn* thing."

107

Chip picked up the pace. "Can you tell us where it came from, Professor? What exactly is it? Are there more of them out there?"

Mister F. shrugged. "To tell you the truth, I don't know. There are tentacles. There are fins. And there's a great deal of inorganic flotsam and jetsam all tangled up in there."

Before Chip could ask another probing – and misleading – question, we all heard a low, muffled, moaning sound. It was a cross between an elk call and a loose fan belt, not very loud, but definitely creepy enough to make the hairs on the back of your neck stand straight up.

Chip jumped on it. "Did you hear that, ladies and gentlemen?" he asked. "Did you hear that, Professor? That sound seemed to come from inside the Monster!"

"I definitely heard something," Mister Fishback said.

"Can we get closer?" Chip knew that this could be an historic TV moment, like when Walter Cronkite announced the death of President Kennedy, or when Neil Armstrong stepped off the LEM and onto the surface of the moon, or when that skier wiped out on *The Wide, Wide World of Sports* and suffered, "the agony of defeat."

That same sound again, much louder this time.

"Something bad is about to happen," Ken said. "Maybe we should high-tail it."

"Good idea," Mihn said.

"Hold on," I lined up a shot. There wasn't much light yet, so I opened the shutter all the way.

As we watched, one end of Mister Fishback's Monster expanded, contracted, and expanded again. But not on its own. Something was inside the thing and trying to get out. Was The Monster giving birth?

Action! I aimed my camera at what appeared to be The Monster's mouth – the part with the most teeth – as something dark and watery came flooding, gushing out. Sea water? Partially coagulated blood? Some other kind of funky secretion? More of that revolting stuff poured out. Gallons of it, turning from dark, to clear, and smelling like deep underwater death and slow, cold rot.

Screams of horror from the crowd. General pandemonium.

"Ladies and gentlemen . . ." Chip's voice was higher, now. "There is something inside the creature." He jumped back, right into Camera Guy, and they both fell to the sand.

Mister Fishback, on the other hand, moved closer to the flood of Monster bilge, investigating, studying it.

My heart was beating as if I'd just run two miles around the Oz track.

People in the crowd yelled and stumbled over each other as they tried to flee the scene.

"I can see something, now!" Chip was back on his feet. "It's round and as large as a bowling ball, pinkish in color, and quivering, dripping with some sort of foul, foamy substance. Can you see it?"

Camera Guy moved in for a close up. Me, too. We bumped into each other.

"Back off, kid," Camera Guy said.

But I kept rolling. This was my flick, after all.

"I see teeth! Grinning teeth!" Chip was nearly screaming, now. "I see eyes! Two eyes, staring right at me!"

To our collective, utter horror, a two-legged creature emerged from inside The Monster. It stood, wobbly and unsure sure of itself, limbs and fingers webbed with bubbled sea slime. Then it spoke. Or tried to. First, it vomited a huge gout of what looked to be a mixture of sea water and squid ink.

And then, the baby monster, pink as a new piglet, and coated in goo and marine corruption, yelled, "Re-elect Tom McCall for Governor! Re-elect Tom McCall for Governor!" and kissed Chip square on the mouth.

Chip responded with a very long and very high shriek of horror and indignation.

Cut! I stopped shooting. So did Camera Guy. Some people laughed, and at least one person booed. The monstrous hatchling – which was actually Mister Richard Trammell – stood there, laughing and dripping and having the time of his life.

The whole story came out the next day in *The Seaport Semaphore,* under the headline, LOCAL MAN PLAYS JONAH PRANK. It seems that Mister Trammell had been watching the late news the night before, and learned that Chip would be in Seaport the next morning to cover the sea monster story. Then, after downing the better part of a jug of his homemade gooseberry wine, Mister Trammell hatched his brazen scheme. Well after midnight, he snuck down to where Mister Fishback's Monster lie dead and fermenting, actually crawled inside the thing, and fell asleep. At dawn, when he heard the Channel Two crew, he thrashed and kicked and yelled and then came crawling out, shouting his praise for Tom McCall.

I'm sure Mister Trammell hoped to get hired by the McCall campaign, and maybe make a few bucks as an official spokesperson – touring the state, making personal appearances, and maybe even snagging a position within the administration. But unfortunately, his idea backfired. For one thing, whatever digestive juices and other bodily fluids and enzymes that still remained inside The Monster had eaten away all of Mister Trammell's hair and beard and bleached his skin pink. And to literally add insult to injury, the McCall campaign folks let it be known on no uncertain terms that they didn't want to be represented by some slime-covered, pale and hairless lunatic. In fact, they threatened legal action if Mister Trammell persisted in his hare-brained plot.

Nobody in Seaport was all that surprised by the story. Nobody that I knew, anyway. We had long ago agreed to let Mister Trammell be Mister Trammell.

Before we left Ono Beach, I decided to get creative, and picked up five or six shots of The Monster from low, tilted angles, like in those European movies. And a close up of that cold, staring eye.

How would I weave these shots into my monster flick? I had no earthly idea, but I didn't care. I was having too much fun living this movie.

# Chapter Seventeen

After a night of scary stories and a morning of old guys climbing out of dead and rotting sea creatures, there was only one place where we could go and sort things out.

"Welcome to Don's Last Stand. May I help you?"

Even after watching The Monster give birth to Richard Trammell, Ken had quite the appetite, and ordered another Hangtown Special. Mihn and I ordered crab burgers.

Before Don went off to rustle up our eats, I had to ask him about Mister Fishback's Monster. "What do you think it is?"

"I know exactly what it is," Don said, "and more importantly, who is responsible."

"Responsible?" I rubbed my hurt shoulder.

"You can't think that big slab is some natural phenomenon," Don said. "Major political powers are at work, here, lads."

"Packwood?" Ken asked.

Bob Packwood was an Oregon senator. I always though he looked a lot like John Agar, star of such cheesy classics as *Women of the Prehistoric Planet* and *Attack of the Puppet People*.

"Nah." Don shook his head. "You're thinking too small. Besides, Packwood is too busy chasing skirts to bother with this kind of thing."

Ken tried again. "Carter, then."

"President Carter?" Mihn asked.

Don winked. "Bull's eye."

"How?" Mihn asked. "Why? He's the president of the United States."

"America is hopelessly addicted to Arab oil," Don said, "that's why."

We agreed. Gas was up to seventy cents a gallon in some places.

"Do we have an alternative energy source?" Don asked.

"Solar power?" Mihn asked. "Wind power?"

"Wrong," Don answered. "There's no profit in that stuff. Nobody can ever own the sun, or buy up all the wind."

Mihn gave it another shot. "Atomic energy?"

"Bingo," Don said. "Before he was president, Carter served with the Naval Reactors Branch, U. S. Atomic Energy Commission. That dead sack of steaming guts and puckered suckers out on Ono Beach is the waste product of some secret government program, better believe it."

"Just like in the movies," I said.

"Just like in the movies," Don said.

*"The creature that had come to Seaport was a horrifying, freak-child of the atom!"*

"Can that kind of thing happen in the United States?" Mihn asked.

Don snickered. "Are you kidding?"

"This is the age of Watergate, after all," Ken said.

"Sock it to me." Don went back to the kitchen.

We wondered and talked until our food arrived. Then we ate and wondered and talked some more. I tapped off a quick shot of Ken, tearing into his Hangtown Special because I knew somehow that the repulsive image would fit into my monster flick.

113

Ken paid for our grub. I just had to ask Don about Moby Dick we hit the road.

"No big mystery," Don said. "The white whale represents the white man's struggle against the dark savage. Put that in your homework assignment. I dare you."

"Will do," I said. Fat chance, I thought.

Out in the parking lot, we saw a car with an Idaho license plate pull up and park.

Ken rubbed his gut and burped. "That was the best beef *chow mein* I've ever had!"

"You can say that again!" I hoped the tourists would hear us and get their stomachs ready for Chinese food. "Those egg rolls were great!"

"No doubt about it!" Mihn had to cover his mouth to keep from laughing that odd Mihn laugh of his.

Then we got out of there, and headed for home.

By the time Ken pulled up in front of our house on Desdemona Street, he had come up with another blockbuster: *The Uncanny Rebirth of Richard Trammell*. "Instant classic," he said.

"A major motion sickness." I grabbed my sleeping bag and eased out of the back seat. "See you guys tomorrow."

"See you," Mihn said.

I went inside. Channel Two reran the story on the five o'clock news that night – but without the part where Chip screamed. It was just as sickening the second time around. And just as hilarious. Dad laughed so hard he didn't make it to the door to relieve his colon. Ma, on the other hand, just shook her head and wondered why the authorities hadn't carted Mister Trammell off a long time ago.

When the news story ended, the TV lady

announced that the mayor of Seaport had declared tomorrow to be Sea Monster Day – and that none other than Tom McCall was on his way to Seaport to make a campaign speech.

"I guess McCall wants the sea monster vote," Ma said.

Then, dinner. Ma's white bread elk burgers. There's something very comforting about eating an animal that your own mother killed.

After we ate, I washed the dishes and told Ma's wooden sea captains about Mister Trammell and The Monster. As they chuckled and shook their heads, I realized that a tiny, wooden version of Mister Trammell would look right at home there on the window sill. When I told the captains that I would be seeing Tom McCall in the morning, they all nodded. Even wooden sea captains loved Mister McCall.

Later, up in my room, I stashed today's film in the closet with the first reel. Then I read about how Tashtego, the Indian harpooner in *Moby Dick*, fell into the blowhole of a whale. I shouldn't have read that particular chapter just before crashing out for the night, because I had a nightmare about being stuck inside the smothering, collapsed digestive tract of some huge, dead beast – maybe it was Mister Fishback's Monster, maybe it wasn't – and being unable to get out. I could feel the smooth ribs and swollen organs inside the animal, smell the stagnant sea water, and actually taste its acidic digestive juices. It was like being buried alive in a smelly, squishy, rotten coffin.

I scratched at the inner walls of the beast, trying to claw my way out, but only filling my hands with mud and slime and chunks of cold gristle. I tried crawling on my belly to escape, just like Mister Trammell had.

115

But after what seemed like hours, I realized I was going the wrong way, and had burrowed more deeply and even more snugly, into the thing. Then I felt thousands of tiny mole crabs, crawling all over me, clicking in their angry mole crab language, and scratching and biting at my legs and arms and face.

Where was Pam Grier when I needed her?

I snapped awake – Hollywood style. I had worked Grandma's quilt into a cocoon around me. At first, I panicked and tried to kick my way free. But my shoulder hurt so badly that I stopped, took a long deep breath, calmed down, and then slowly unwrapped myself.

I got out of bed, went down the hall with my pillow, and lay down on the floor in front of Steph's room. I honestly wanted to go inside, tell her all about what had happened today, and about my bad dream, but I fell asleep.

# Chapter Eighteen

## Wednesday

It was "The Dream Police," by Cheap Trick, this time.

The Thunderbird pulled up. Ken stuck his head out the window. "Nice day for politics," he said. "A little sun. A little breeze."

*"It was a perfect day – for horror!"*

"We'll see." Armed with my camera and a fresh roll of film, I jogged around to the other side of the car and hopped in behind Mihn.

"I am anxious to see the American political system at work," Mihn said.

Zomb took a twitching perch on my shoulder. He gave off a very powerful, very familiar smell. "Pine Sol?" I asked.

"That stupid mongrel found a dead nutria, and just had to roll in it," Ken said. "Then Granny washed him with dish soap and Pine Sol."

Poor Zomb. He never got a break.

And then we were off to Ono Beach.

By now, *The Seaport Semaphore* had asked its readers to come up with a name for the steaming pile, rotting away on Ono Beach. Among the more creative entries submitted:

The Seaport Sea Serpent
The Big Creepy
The Poseidon Misadventure
Captain Crunch's Revenge
The winning entry, as determined by the editorial

panel of the paper: Moby Ick. A timely choice, I suppose, considering Ms. Ellerath's reading assignment. But I still liked the name Mister Fishback's Monster best because I thought Mister F. deserved some credit for his pre-dawn discovery.

But whatever the name, Tom McCall was coming to see it today. And Seaport was ready for the historic event. As we cruised through town, I was amazed by what folks had put together on such short notice. Banners hung across the streets. Little kids wore mom-made sea monster costumes and growled at each other. Store windows had snarling octopi and snapping sea dragons painted on their insides. There were car washes and cake walks and T-shirts, and the Orpheum Theater was showing *The Crater Lake Monster,* a low-budget, dinosaur attacks movie that was filmed in California, not Oregon, for twenty-five cents a ticket.

Along the way, I squeezed off a few quick, moving shots of the festivities, even though I still wasn't quite sure how I would be able to put it all together. But something told me to save film for McCall's big speech, and maybe, hopefully, something even more spectacular.

*"It was an eerie, ominous premonition!"*

We passed Seaport Pharmacy, where Mister Trammell, his pink skin peeling like old house paint, and hairless as the day he was born, was selling autographed pictures of himself for five bucks a throw. People were actually lining up. By this time, though, Mister Trammell had decided to support Tom McCall's opponent, Vic Atiyeh.

I remembered what the old man had said about judgment.

Ono Beach. High noon. There were at least two

hundred cars up in the parking lot, with license plates from all up and down the west coast. It seemed to me as if Seaport was just asking for trouble. And you know what happens when you ask for trouble. The Channel Two News van was there, too. No sign of Chip, though. I thought after being goo-kissed by Mister Trammell, Chip had apparently gone back to Portland, vowing never to return.

Ken found a parking place. Down on the beach, Mister Fishback's Monster looked bloated this morning, more like a tightly stuffed bratwurst, now, than a burrito.

*"Was the cryptic creature going through some kind of bizarre metamorphosis?*

The Seaport High School Band was warming up on one side of The Monster. Cheerleaders practiced a routine on the other. At the top of the beach, a viewing stand had been built for the soon-to-arrive governor. In between The Monster and the viewing stand, hundreds of people were unfolding their beach chairs and spreading out their beach blankets and snapping film cartridges into their cheap plastic cameras.

I grabbed a quick master shot of the scene. Maybe ten feet of film. "Let's get down there," I said, "while we can."

On the way down to the sand, ribbons and balloons and hand painted signs lined the trail on either side of us. "This feels like a circus," I said.

"More like a freak show," Ken said.

"This will be fun," Mihn said. "I have never seen a governor before."

"Ex-governor," Ken said.

When we got down to the beach, the band was warmed up and ready to perform. The cheerleaders,

119

waiting in frozen, smiling formation, now, looked like they belonged in a wax museum. Or a morgue.

*"They were dead, but alive!"*

"Check it out." Ken pointed – to where Don had parked his grill on wheels, and was now busy slinging grub and selling it at twice the usual price. "And look who's with him."

It was Ronny Behr, scrubbing pots behind Don's grill. My shoulder burned all of a sudden, and for just a second, I wanted to run back up to Ken's white Thunderbird – and safety. But I held my ground.

"Must be part of his sentence for breaking into Don's," Ken said.

"Maybe he will change his bully ass ways," Mihn said.

Just then, Ronny looked up, saw me, and ran a finger across his throat.

"I wouldn't count on it," I said.

"Don't worry," Ken said. "Don's got him under control."

I wanted to be as close to the action as possible. We found a spot in front of the viewing stand, and kneeled in the cold sand.

Photographers must think alike, because none other than Channel Two Camera Guy himself set up right next to me. "Stay out of my way, kid," he said.

"Let's keep it professional," I said. Ken was next to me, so I felt brave enough to be a wise ass.

The band started playing the official Oz fanfare. The cheerleaders came to perky life, and started their routine.

"Here come de Gov." Ken pointed.

Sure enough, Tom McCall was on his way down the path to the beach, wearing a tweed jacket, and displaying his usual, confident smile.

120

People applauded and cheered.

The former governor wasn't alone. The mayor of Seaport was with him, along with several other Oregon big shots, including Les Schwab himself — wearing his trademark cowboy hat, tilted at a slight angle. Another member of the entourage stood out from the other VIP's. He wore a cape, for one thing.

"I don't believe it," I said. "Professor Ravenswort!"

"Professor?" Mihn asked. "Where does he teach?"

"On TV," I said.

The celebs waved to the folks and smiled, and then they sat down on metal chairs behind a lectern. The band stopped, the cheerleaders turned into frozen corpses once again, and Mayor Hanford stepped up to speak.

Polite applause.

"Good morning, Seaporters, visitors, and friends." Hanford smoothed his comb-over. "And thank you all for being here on this beautiful day here on the Oregon Coast."

"Windbag," Ken said.

"Ken . . ." Mihn was actually paying attention.

"It is my great pleasure to introduce a great man, statesman, and activist," Hanford said. "Please join me in welcoming the once and future governor of the great state of Oregon, Mister Tom McCall!"

Genuine applause this time. People liked this man. I clapped, too. So did Ken and Mihn. Mister McCall stood and shook hands with the mayor. Then he put on a pair of horn rims, took some papers out of his pocket, and spread them flat on the lectern. I raised my camera and squinted into the view finder.

Action! "So tell me." Mister McCall nodded to The Monster. "What kind of bait did you use to land this thing?"

Real laughter. Then someone shouted an answer: "We used a tourist from California! Works every time!"

More sincere laughs, applause – and a loud ripping sound.

"What was that?" Mihn asked.

I immediately, instinctively whipped my camera toward The Monster, and kept shooting as it shook and rippled from one end to the other. Then the giant bratwurst seemed to shrink, a little at first, and then a lot, as an enormous but invisible bubble of deep gut fermentation erupted from one puckered orifice or another, accompanied by what sounded for all the world like the off-key blaring and blatting of a dozen poorly tuned oboes – and the sharp, pungent, and overpowering odor of furthest down, Neptunian rot and putrefaction.

That stink hit me in the back of the throat, strangled my uvula, and then crawled up behind my nose and made me gag. I wasn't the only one. There were groans from the audience. Choking sounds. Folks covered their noses and mouths.

*"The raw stench had a personality, a clutching, grasping life of its own!"*

Ken quoted one of his favorite songs: "We've got to get out of this place!"

Mihn looked sick, now. "I cannot breathe!"

"Go ahead without me." I mashed my nose into the back of the camera, held my breath, and kept rolling. I had to get tough and capture this disgusting event on film. My audience was depending on me. "I'm staying!"

And then it started for real.

Somewhere behind me, toward the back of the

crowd, up close to The Monster, somebody retched. It was a deep, guttural sound, the kind of sound you only hear in emergency rooms and on roller coasters. It was a retch, but it was a dry retch. I kept shooting. I knew that this was merely a prelude, an overture to something worse.

Sure enough, someone else, a kid this time, actually vomited – really let go. Breakfast from this morning, dinner from last night, a candy bar or two. It all came hurtling out at the speed of sound. A little old lady, someone's grandmother, no doubt, came next. Her dentures hit the sand before her partially digested English muffin, marmalade, and tea. I felt bad for her. Another kid blew. And then the inevitable chain reaction began.

*"It was a reflexive, contagious, avalanche of gastric horror!"*

One person after another, both young and old, tourist and resident, either bent and heaved into the sand, or spouted high into the air. I panned from one puker to the next,

Mihn fell victim. He hadn't eaten as much, so his upchuck wasn't at all noteworthy.

Ken on the other hand, a big eater, launched a head-back-and-howling arch of semi-digested food that may or may not have included a Hangtown Special or two.

Camera Guy bent over and pitched a creamy gutful.

Weakling, I thought. Punk. So far, I had managed to hold down my breakfast and keep shooting.

Don had his back to me when he blew. But I got a good angle of Ronny with his hand clamped tight over his mouth – and spewing through his nostrils. Must've hurt.

I remained unaffected. How do you keep your

gorge down when everyone around you is puking their intestines inside out? You hold your breath and think of the most stomach-calming things you can bring to mind – like your Ma's blackberry pie, freshly baked, with vanilla ice cream melting on top of it. Or her barbecued salmon steaks. Or her two-cheese fondue. And so those were the things that I thought about as the barf-alanche rolled over the assembled throng to where the VIP's stood, horror-struck and helpless. Then it seemed to hover for a brief moment – just like the wave in that famous Japanese print – before slamming down with all its nauseastic force.

I remembered the spicy tang of Ma's venison chili. I could almost taste her Crab Louie with black olives as I stepped over the convulsing Camera Guy, and up to the viewing stand as the mayor, then McCall, and then Professor Ravenswort, lost whatever expensive breakfast they had eaten before coming to town. Coffee and sweet rolls, apparently. Maybe some scrambled eggs. Bacon. It was hard to tell. Les Schwab removed that famous cowboy hat – and roar-puked directly into it.

Very obviously, this was not the photo opportunity everyone had been hoping for.

Ah, Ma's strawberry shortcake. I kept filming and remembering Ma's best cooking until I was nearly out of film, and then I panned one hundred and eighty degrees back to the very source of the stink, Mister Fishback's Monster – which looked smaller, now – and held the shot steady. But then, just when I thought I had made it, just when I thought my bizarre imagining skills had saved me, all I could think about was the one dish in Ma's repertoire that I didn't like: her tuna casserole.

Canned tuna, of course. Chinese noodles. Mayo, I

think. All baked together in the same rectangular dish. Soupy. Nasty. It was all I could think about, now, no matter how hard I tried to think of something, anything else. Luckily, just as I remembered that final, gag-inducing ingredient: cream of mushroom soup, I ran out of film.

Cut! And then I lost it, too, vomiting so hard that my glasses fell off, and simultaneously composing the first haiku ever devoted to puke.

*I see it all, now:*
*My breakfast, lunch and dinner.*
*When did I eat corn?*

# Chapter Nineteen

Ono Beach was like a battlefield – spattered and puddled, not with blood, but with partially digested food and bile. As if that stretch of beach wasn't nasty and smelly enough what with Mister Fishback's Monster, and all. But nobody had been hurt or killed. Most folks were still on their knees, either holding their stomachs and shaking their heads, or comforting their green-gilled kids, or quietly dry heaving one last time.

There was no sign of McCall. No sign of Hanford. They had abandoned us in our hour of nauseous need. No sign of Professor Ravenswort, either. I didn't hold it against him, though. He was an entertainer, after all, not a leader.

"Are you all right?" Ken came low crawling over to me, pulling Mihn with him like a wounded foxhole buddy.

"Yeah," I said. "I'm OK."

"What was that ass?" Mihn looked weak and limp.

"Vomin-o effect," Ken said, as if he were the wrinkle-nosed veteran of some similar gastric upheaval.

"Let's get out of here and into some fresh air," Mihn croaked. *"Please!"*

"Don't worry, buddy." Ken was in full hero mode. "I'll get you up to the parking lot for some air. You coming, Steve?"

"I'll catch up with you guys in a little while."

"Good luck." Ken dragged Mihn to safety.

126

When I felt up to it, I started up the trail to the parking lot. I was still a little weak in the knees myself, and, as any beachcomber knows, walking in loose sand can tire you out faster than walking on hard pavement. I knew there was a concrete bench about half way up the trail, and I needed to take a break.

But when I arrived at the bench, someone was already there. He was an old man, thin – no, skinny – birdlike, wearing black dress pants, a sweat-drenched T-shirt, and the kind of straw hat that people wear to protect themselves from the sun. (You don't see too many of those in Oregon.)

I thought maybe the old man was in trouble. "Sir? Are you OK?"

The old man looked up. His face was long, and his cheeks were hollow, like John Carradine, or Raymond Massey. I knew right away who he was.

"I'm fine," Professor Ravenswort said – in a somewhat quieter, less theatrical version of that *Creature Feature* voice. "Thank you for checking on me, though. You look wrung out yourself. Sit down."

This was another once in a lifetime opportunity, so I took the professor up on his offer.

"That was quite the show down there." The professor nodded to my movie camera. "Did you get it all on film?"

It felt good to sit. "Yes, I did – in blazing eight millimeter. But I'm not sure what I'll do with all the footage."

"Footage? You know your terminology. Do you make movies?"

I was usually embarrassed to answer the question. Not this time, though. "That's right."

"Is that what you want to do as a career?"

"I want to do special effects – especially stop

motion."

"That's a tough game to break into. Do you have plan?"

The breeze felt good, and it didn't smell – as much, now. "There's a film school in Portland. I hope I can enroll there after I graduate high school."

"I used to work in the industry," Professor Ravenswort said. "Back before you were born, I'm sure." If he knew that I knew who he was, he didn't let on. "I was a studio projectionist, you know, that nameless, faceless guy up in the booth, screening film for the execs."

"Which studio did you work for? Universal? MGM?"

The professor laughed. "No. I worked for the cheap outfits, East Coast studios you've probably never heard of. I eventually did some voice work, though. Foreign art films, mostly, dubbing English dialogue. I did a few coming attractions here and there, too."

"You mean trailers?"

The professor smiled. "I truly believe that the most talented people in the picture business are the folks that cut trailers together."

"How come?"

"They take the worst turkey imaginable, glue together the best three minutes, add some corny narration, and presto, you can't wait to see that movie. It's cinematic alchemy."

"Movies are magic," I said.

"Pure magic."

We laughed and we talked about good movies and bad movies, and when the conversation lagged, I asked the professor about the white whale. I wanted to know his opinion. "It's for my language arts class."

He thought for a moment before answering. "The whale is white so that snobby critics and language arts teachers can fill in any far out meaning they want to in order to feel like geniuses."

I liked that answer. "Makes sense to me."

"Just a thought," Professor Ravenswort said, and then he stood. "Well, I'd better get out of here and back on the road. I've got a long drive back to Portland."

"I've got to get going, too," I said.

"Good luck in Hollywood," the professor said, and he actually meant it. "Believe in yourself. Stick up for yourself."

"I will."

"Be confident. Don't let anyone beat you down."

"I know."

We shook. The professor's hand was bony, but strong. I didn't ask for an autograph. He didn't offer one. And that was OK.

"Just one more thing," Professor Ravenswort said.

"What's that?"

That wise, kind smile faded. "Keep a close eye on the film you shot today. Don't let anybody have it."

# -Part Three-

"Though in many of its aspects this visible world seems formed in love, the invisible spheres were formed in fright."
— ***Moby Dick***, **Herman Melville, 1851**

"WHAT WAS THE THING NATURE HAD SPAWNED ON THE OCEAN FLOOR?"
— **Poster,** *The Phantom from 10,000 Leagues*, **1955**

"Without a reason why
You've blown it all sky high."
— **"Sky High," by Jigsaw, 1975**

"Oh, the humanity!"
— **Herbert Morrison, eyewitness to the crash of the Hindenburg, 1937**

# Chapter Twenty

Ken and Mihn were in the Thunderbird, waiting for me. Zombie was sitting up in the backseat, panting, his furry, scarred mug pressed up against the window, and waiting for me, too. Ken looked none the worse for stinky, pukey wear. In fact, he looked oddly refreshed, and with plenty of room for a Hangtown Special. But Mihn's eyes were closed and his mouth was open and gasping, and he looked like a dying carp.

"You OK?" I asked.

"No." Mihn's head rolled slowly to the side and opened his eyes. "I feel ass empty."

I held up my camera like a trophy. "I got the whole disgusting episode on film, every heave, every Ralph, Roger and Earl! Not only that, I actually met Professor Ravenswort on the way back up here, and I talked to him!"

"Good for you." Ken gunned the Bird. "Let's get out of this stink hole and get some fresh air moving in the car."

Mihn moaned. "Fresh air . . ."

I climbed over the slowly recuperating Mihn, got in the back with my good buddy, Zombie, hugged that nasty, stitched-together ferret, and took in a deep nose full of Pine Sol. "What a relief!" Zomb shivered and licked my face and seemed glad to be appreciated for a change.

We rolled down all the windows. Then, accompanied by Journey's "Wheel in the Sky," we left barf-soaked, chunk-strewn, malodorous Ono Beach. The smell of death faded almost immediately, but it still lingered somewhere up at the back of my nasal cavity, so I held Zombie even closer.

"Hey, man." Ken sounded like one of the hippies that Dad hated so much. "Pass me that ferret. Let me take a hit off that."

"No way, man" I said. "You get your own ferret."

"That *is* my ferret," Ken said. "I raised him from a puppy, or whatever it is you call baby ferrets."

"You call them hobs," Mihn said. "Baby ferrets are called hobs."

I passed Zombie up to the front seat. "Don't Bogart it."

Ken took a hit, held it, exhaled. "Primo." Then he passed the ferret to Mihn. "Here, man."

But Mihn abstained. "No thank you." He passed Zombie back to me. "Do you suppose all of that barfing was what Mister Trammell meant when he talked about the bitter blood of judgment?"

"Beats me," I said.

"Bile is bitter," Ken said.

Mihn gagged a little when he heard that.

Just after we merged onto the Coast Highway, Ken uttered yet another line of classic B-movie dialogue: "I think we're being followed."

"Followed?" I looked out the back window of the T-Bird. Sure enough, the Channel Two News van was right behind us. Chip Boost was in the front passenger seat. My cinematic nemesis, Camera Guy, was driving.

"What the ass do they want?" Mihn asked.

Zombie snarled and his runaway eye spun in its

134

socket like a roulette wheel.

"Should I lose 'em?" Ken sat up straight. "I can lose 'em, you know. Prepare for evasive maneuvers!" Then he started doing that sound effect from a dozen submarine movies. "Ahooga! Ahooga!"

"Wait!" I said, "I don't think Chip wants to hurt anybody."

Ken calmed down. "Are you sure?"

"He must be a good man," Mihn said. "He is on TV."

We proceeded to our house on Desdemona Street. Ken parked the Bird out front. The Channel Two van pulled up behind us.

We all got out of our respective vehicles. It felt like a showdown in an old western. A standoff. There were no blowing tumbleweeds, but I could almost hear that whistling theme music from *The Good, the Bad, and the Ugly*.

Mihn stood at my side, like my Vietnamese deputy. "I do not like this," he said.

"Don't worry." Ken stood behind us. "If things get weird, I'll just mess up Chip's hair."

"Here." I passed my camera to Ken. "Just in case."

But he wouldn't take it. "Keep it," he said. "It's perfectly safe with you."

"Thanks." I appreciated Ken's faith in me.

"Hello fellas." Chip introduced himself. Up close, that gleaming TV smile was almost creepy. I had to wonder if the reporter had been horribly mangled, and then re-assembled in some underground network laboratory.

Chip and I shook hands. "I'm Steve. These are my friends, Mihn, and Ken."

"Glad to meet you." Chip looked incomplete

without a microphone in his hand. "Were you guys on the beach during McCall's press conference?"

"You mean the great, heaving chuck-a-thon show?" Ken asked.

Mihn stepped forward. "Maybe we were there. Then again, maybe we were not." He stepped back.

"You were there." Chip nodded to my camera. "And you captured the whole thing on film."

"We scooped ya," Ken said. "Unlike your boy, here, Steve managed to hold his mud and filmed every disgusting second of it."

Camera Guy looked like he still had a queasy stomach.

"I guess you did." Chip shot Camera Guy a disapproving glance. "How would you like to see your film on Channel Two?"

"Channel Two?" The idea caught me off guard. "TV?"

"How much are you willing to pay?" Mihn asked.

"I'm sorry," Chip said. "We don't pay for amateur footage."

"Amateur?" Ken growled. "Steve is a pro shooter. He's going to Hollywood after he graduates, ya know."

"Hollywood?" Chip grinned. "So, you want to make movies?"

"That's right," I said. "I'm going to make movies."

Camera Guy chuckled.

"OK," Chip said. "Fifty bucks. That's money out of my own pocket."

Fifty bucks? Was that enough money? Was it too much? I wasn't sure. Didn't those two California guys make a boatload of baksheesh for the Bigfoot film they shot a few years earlier? I turned to my friends

136

for guidance. Mihn shook his head. Ken just glared at Chip through those moronic, but admittedly intimidating goggles of his.

"One hundred dollars," Chip said, upping the ante, now. "And screen credit, if the story goes on the air."

Screen credit and a hundred bucks?

"Bear in mind," Chip said. "This story could go national."

"National?" I asked. "You mean Walter Cronkite?"

Chip shook his head. "Cronkite is CBS. But don't think for one minute that Howard K. Smith is some second stringer."

It was too much for me to take in. "I need some time to think."

"I'll give you until ten o'clock tomorrow morning." Chip handed me his business card. "I'm staying in town tonight, just in case something else happens. After tomorrow, nobody will give a crap."

Hmmm. Could this be my big break? "Will I get the film back when you're done with it?"

"No," Chip said. "It will become property of Channel Two News, in perpetuity."

"That means forever," Camera Guy said. I didn't like the idea of giving up my film – and I guess it showed.

"OK. One hundred and fifty dollars for the film," Chip said. "And screen credit."

"Are you kidding me?" Camera Guy couldn't believe it.

Neither could I. One hundred and fifty dollars? That was a sizeable chunk of change. And I could almost see my name spelled out at the bottom of the TV screen.

Chip: "Final offer."

Camera Guy: "Take the money, kid."

But I needed more time to decide, that's all. "I'll call you in the morning."

Chip shook his head. "I think you're making a big mistake."

"These proceedings are closed," Ken said, quoting General MacArthur during the Japanese surrender in 1945. He shooed Chip and Camera Guy back to their van. "Don't call us, we'll call you."

Chip waved to us as the news van drove off. Camera Guy didn't wave or even look our way. Then it was just the three of us, standing there on Desdemona Street.

"What should I do?"

"To sell your film, or not to sell your film," Ken said. "That is the freakin' question."

"One hundred and fifty dollars is an ass lot of money," Mihn said.

"This could get your foot inside the Hollywood door," Ken said.

I looked down at my clunky old movie camera. "I know. I know."

"Ass!" Mihn pointed to the Thunderbird – where Zombie was clawing and whining at the window again. His right eyeball was totally white.

"Mother of pearl!" Ken said. "Zombie's eye is stuck again. I gotta get him back to Granny so she can fix him."

"I think I will call it a day, too," Mihn said. "I still feel weak from all that vomiting."

"Me, too," I said. "I've got some thinking to do. I'll call you guys tomorrow."

Ken and Mihn got back in the car and drove off,

accompanied by the song, "Carry On, Wayward Son," by the group Boston.

I went in the house – and was shocked to see that Ma and Dad were standing at the front window. Ma had her skates on for some reason. The folks had seen and heard everything. They were a little fuzzy about the VIP puke party, so I filled them in.

"And Chip wants to buy your film?" Dad asked.

"A hundred and fifty dollars," Ma said. "That's a lot of money for a dorky kid."

"I could buy a super eight camera with that money," I said. "Zoom lens. Sound, maybe. What do you think I should do?"

"I'd go for it," Dad said. "But this is your decision, Junior."

"A hundred and fifty bucks . . ." Ma shook her head.

"I need to brush my teeth after all that puking." I headed upstairs to the bathroom, but I didn't get very far.

"Hey, check it out." Dad said. "There's a whop-daddy Caddy parked right in front of the house."

I came back down and looked outside. Dad was right. The Cadillac was black and the windows were tinted so we couldn't see who was inside. The engine was running.

"I know just about every car in town," Dad said, "but I don't recognize that one."

We watched the black Caddy for a while. I held my camera close.

"Something's up," Dad said, "something shady."

*"A four-wheeled intruder had come to Desdemona Street. Who drove that ominous vehicle? What did they want?"*

"That's enough!" Still wearing her heavy skates, Ma clunk-stomped out the front door. Then, tucked low and ready to slam, she went sailing down our driveway and onto Desdemona Street.

Dad and I ran after her.

"Show yourselves, you low-ball cowards!" Ma rolled up to the driver-side window of the mysterious black Cadillac, like some pissed-off carhop, and started banging on the dark windshield. "Who are you? What do you want?"

The Caddy peeled out, swung hard to port, and left Ma shaking her fist and yelling.

Dad and I caught up. "Did you get the license number?" Dad was a little out of breath.

Ma spun on her skates. "There were no plates on that car!"

"No plates? That's illegal!" Dad was confused.

But the situation seemed perfectly obvious to me. "Somebody else wants my film."

*Who wanted that flickering eight millimeter film? And just how far would they go to get it?*

# Chapter Twenty-One

## Thursday Morning

I brushed my teeth, gave Steph a quick, whispered update, and went to my room. I should've hidden today's film right away, but I was worn out, so I put my movie camera on my driftwood desk without thinking about it. Then I read from *Moby Dick* for a while. I still had no clue as to why the whale was white.

Liver and onions for dinner. I know, I know. But Ma could make even fried liver taste good. I think it had something to do with onion soup mix.

After dinner, I watched TV with Ma and Dad. Then I went to up to my room to crash after a weird day. I hit the lights, pushed the window open about a fourth of the way, and listened to Pam until I fell asleep.

*"Clear skies tonight.*
*West winds at five to seven knots."*

I didn't dream about anything scary or funny. I didn't dream about Julie Smith, either. But sometime around midnight, I must have heard something. Some creak or click or squeak, something more than just the usual noise of the house settling. And something more than just Pam Grier's comforting, not-gonna-take-no-mess voice.

*"Tomorrow:*

141

*Partly cloudy."*

I woke up to see a dark, hulking shadow, right outside my bedroom window – and looking in at me. I instantly recognized that silhouette. There was no doubt about it. It was one of the tall, fuzzy-suited, bulb-eyed and laughably unrealistic Martian soldiers from *Invaders from Mars.*

*"Invaders from Mars – capturing humans at will for their own sinister purposes!"*

This wasn't a movie, or a dream, or a Steve-O-Scopic figment of my imagination. Or was it? It was getting to the point where I couldn't tell right away. Either way, real or not, I was too scared to move.

Why hadn't Pam warned me about shaggy, B-movie Martians? Why was she still rambling on about the weather?

*"Calm seas.*

*Wind waves at four to seven feet."*

The Martian slowly opened the window the rest of the way. Moonlight glinted off his head and shoulders and bulging eyes.

I wanted to hide under Grandma's quilt, but I knew that if I did, the intruding Martian would be that much closer when I peeked out.

*"Chance of rain."*

The big fuzzy Martian crawled across the windowsill and onto my desk, almost bumping the camera – which had a hundred and fifty dollars' worth of Ono Beach film coiled inside it. That's when I realized that this was actually happening, and that the Martian was after my film!

The Martian turned off my radio, climbed down from my desk, and accidentally knocked my copy of *Moby Dick* onto the floor.

142

I gathered up all my energy and gave myself a five second countdown. At the end of that time, I would bounce out of bed and to the door without even touching the ground, and then tear down the stairs — faster than the legendary side hill dodger – to safety.

Five . . .

The Martian soldier stood, tall, scary — and smelling, for some odd reason, like Old Spice.

Four . . .

The Martian started going through the drawers of my driftwood desk, no doubt searching for a reel of some kind, but not knowing that the film he was looking for hadn't been developed yet and was resting quietly right there inside the camera. Then, somehow realizing that I was awake, the Martian slowly turned his beetle-eyed head in my direction.

Three . . .

The Martian ran at me, put one hand over my mouth, the other hand on my throat, and spoke – in Earth English. "Where is the film?"

I was paralyzed with fear, just like in the movies. I couldn't breathe, let alone call for help.

"Where is the film you shot, shit bird?"

I remembered what Ken had said about protecting my flick, balled up my skinny fist, and punched the trespassing Martian right in those buggy eyes – which then broke in two and fell off because they were actually plastic safety glasses. "You can't have it!"

My bed broke. The Martian fell on top of me, and his hands pressed down hard on my face and throat. It hurt, but that pain made me really mad, and since a good cowboy movie punch hadn't done the trick, I decided to inflict as much pain as I could. So I stuck both of my index fingers in the Martian's nose, and pushed. Hard as I could.

143

The Martian yelled and cussed. He punched me in the chest, and pushed off me. Then, as he staggered back toward the window, he stopped, and stared at my movie camera. "There it is!"

My bedroom door blew open and banged against the wall. Dad came running in, wearing only his boxer shorts and a T-shirt that said LAGUNA SURF CLUB. Dad hit the lights – and he jumped back a little when he saw the Martian, who was actually a human in blue, mechanic's coveralls – and halfway out the window by then.

Now, Ma, hair in braids and wearing one of her Seaport Sharks jerseys, was in my room, armed with "Hondo," her favorite twelve-gauge shotgun, and yelling, "Freeze, pervert!" She jacked a round.

But the Martian was gone by then.

"We heard a noise," Dad said.

I pointed to my copy of *Moby Dick*, there on the floor.

"Gonna bag me a pee-do-phile!" Ma ran out of my room and down the stairs.

"Be right back!" Dad followed Ma.

I crawled out of my broken bed and over to my open window. I saw Ma, down on Desdemona Street and running after the man in coveralls – who was just then diving into the back seat of a big black Cadillac with tinted windows and no license plates.

Ma T-stopped and adopted a good firing stance. The Caddy peeled out. Ma let go with both barrels. Blammo! Sparks flew up from the back of the Cadillac. Dad came up behind Ma, passed her, running after the Cadillac, and yelling. Ma warned him to get out of her line of fire. Dad complied, but by that time, the Caddy was well out of shotgun range.

144

Upstairs, I had almost caught my breath. I remembered my camera. "The film!" I said the words in a scratchy voice. I'd been choked, after all. But the camera was there on my desk, safe and unopened. I put a hand to my throat and couldn't help but think that maybe I should've taken Chip's money.

The folks came back to check on me. "Did you get a good look at the perp's face?" Ma asked.

I picked up those broken safety glasses. "No, but I'm sure it wasn't Chip the reporter." Then I wondered if Camera Guy had just paid me a visit. I knew he didn't like me. I had managed to film the beach puke-tacular after he had succumbed to the stink-nami and missed it.

Dad picked up my movie camera and turned it over in his hands. "Could something else have happened at Ono Beach, something maybe you didn't notice at the time?

"Like what?" I asked. Had there been UFO's in the sky today? Had Jimmy Hoffa's body bobbed to the surfaced just off shore? Had I endangered national security, somehow?

"Whatever happened," Dad said, "somebody doesn't want that film to see the light of day."

Ma called the cops. The sheriff came out, took a report. I took the film out of the camera, canned it, and stashed the film can in the closet with the first two reels. Then I finally went to back to bed – with my bedroom window locked, and Ma and Hondo camped outside my door. Just in case.

I dreamed about a slow-moving, sinister, black Cadillac, with demonic eyes instead of headlights. Captain Ahab was driving it, steering with one hand and holding a harpoon outside the driver's side window with the other.

145

None other than Tom McCall was in the backseat.
Tom McCall as a villain?
Weird.

# Chapter Twenty-Two

**Thursday Morning**

I had a black eye. My shoulder still burned from being punched. And now, I had a sore neck from being goon-choked by a Martian. What kind of injury would I receive today?

Decisions, decisions. I hadn't made up my mind about the film, which seemed all the more valuable after what happened last night. Wouldn't it be safer to just give the reel to Chip, take the money, and maybe get my name out there? The odds of me getting into the big-time movie business were slim enough as it was. I was going to need some kind of break sooner or later. Why not now? I didn't want a career making driver's education films, after all. What a thought.

On the other hand, I had three reels of amazing footage: a scary Monster, colorful local characters, puking politicians, a Coast Guard chopper, and a pretty girl. Close ups. Master shots. Tilted, European camera angles. And for some uncanny, back-of-my-brain reason, I felt certain that it was all going to fall together in perfect cinematic order, and that I'd have something special, something totally unique, to show to the long hairs at the film school over in Portland.

I took a shower and got dressed. Before I went downstairs, I put my hand on Stephanie's door.

"What should I do, Steph?" I didn't explain my

two choices. My twin sister knew what had happened, knew all the pros and cons. My sister knew me. And she knew what I needed to do.

Then I went downstairs. Ma and Dad were in the kitchen. Ma had her skates on again. I guess she was breaking in a new pair. I passed the folks, and headed to the family room to check the TV and see if anything else had gone on at Ono Beach, half-hoping that the Pacific Ocean had re-claimed The Monster in the night and that my very own monster movie was over.

There was nothing on television. But Mister Fishback's Monster was still there, I was sure. I could feel it.

I joined Ma and Dad for breakfast: Swiss and crab omelettes, and fried potatoes. I didn't say anything. Neither did Dad. But I guess Ma couldn't stand it any longer.

"Well?" she asked.

I acted like I didn't know what she was talking about. "Well, what?"

"Are you going to sell your movie film," she asked, "or not?" I knew Ma wanted me to go for the money.

I looked at Dad. He was looking at me, chewing slowly.

Then I looked over at Ma's sea captain collection and all those sure, stern, wood carved faces. They all agreed with Steph. No doubt about it. So I swallowed a salt and peppered mouthful of Ma's fried potatoes, and just said it: "I'm going to keep my film."

Dad smiled and resumed chewing at normal speed.

"There goes a hundred and fifty dollars," Ma said. "How many lawns would you have to mow in order

**148**

to . . ?"

I held up my hand and cut Ma off. "We've decided."

"We?" Ma started in again – twice. But each time, I just put up my hand and stopped her cold. This was my film, and I would live with the consequences. I felt good. Strong. Right, for a change.

I finished eating and got up from the table. I called Chip at his hotel, told him about getting throttled by a Martian – and that I had decided not to sell my film.

"Are you sure?" Chip asked.

"I'm sure," I said.

There was a long silence on the other end of the phone. "Now, listen," Chip said. "I don't want to scare you, and this isn't a bluff, but somebody wants that film. Somebody big. Somebody powerful. You don't know who you're dealing with."

"Do you know who I'm dealing with? Do they drive a black Cadillac?"

"Be careful," Chip said. Then he hung up.

"OK." I stood there, staring at the phone, listening to the dial tone and wondering. Was I in some sort of Abraham Zapruder, eight millimeter danger?

"What did Chip say?" Dad asked.

I hung up. "He told me to be careful."

"Careful?" Ma asked. "Careful of what?"

"He wouldn't say."

"I want to see what's on that film," Dad said. "We need to get it developed, but I don't think we should take it to those shutter-chucks at Seaport Pharmacy."

"That's the only place in town that processes eight millimeter," I said.

"Go get your film." Dad went to the phone, and started dialing. "I know exactly where to go."

I ran upstairs and paused at Steph's door. "Thanks for your help," I said. "I'll talk to you later."

Dad yelled from downstairs. "Let's get a move on, Junior!"

I went to my room and snagged my film cans.

Two minutes later, Dad and I were back in the bus, on the way to – somewhere. There were three film cans under my seat.

*"This was a mission, an adventure, for a heroic man and his brave son!"*

"I know who a man who can keep your film from . . ." and then Dad actually said the words. ". . . falling into the wrong hands."

I had to laugh. This was a blast! I checked at the rear view mirror. "Do you see any black Cadillacs back there?"

Dad chuckled. "Those yipe-holes won't be driving a Cadillac this time. No way. They'll be driving something less conspicuous."

"Like a Pacer?"

"Maybe."

A convoy of Army trucks and jeeps passed us, headed toward Ono Beach. I would've grabbed a few feet of film – for cheap realism, but I didn't have a camera with me on this trip.

"National Guard," Dad said. "Army Corps of Engineers." He turned on the radio.

Radio News Lady: "The governor has tasked the Oregon National Guard with the disposal of the so-called monster. According to sources, dynamite will be used to blow it out to sea so that marine scavengers can consume what's left of it. This will occur on Saturday morning at nine o'clock."

"That's what I thought," Dad said.

Radio News Lady: "But at least one member of the local community is against the demolition, and he is here with us today. Ronald Fishback is a science teacher at Oswald West High School. He found the dead creature. In fact, some people have named the dead thing in his honor."

"It's Mister Fishback!" I turned up the volume.

"That guy gets around," Dad said.

"Tell me, Mister Fishback," Radio News Lady asked, "what do you think about your monster and the upcoming demolition?"

"I am dead set against it." It was Mister Fishback's voice, all right. "We still don't know what this object is or where it came from."

"Did you read about Tom McCall's press conference yesterday? Hundreds of people were made violently ill."

"I realize that," Mister F. said. "On the other hand, there's so much we could learn by dissecting the thing, studying it."

Radio News Lady laughed. "You sound like a scientist in a nineteen fifties horror movie."

But Mister Fishback was serious. "Oregon State sent two graduate students to examine the thing, but I don't think they did a very thorough investigation. I did my own examination, my own research. I have my own theory about the dead thing on Ono Beach, and if I'm right, everyone along the West Coast could be in danger."

Theory? Danger? But before Mister Fishback could elaborate, Radio News Lady broke for a Les Schwab commercial. And we had arrived.

"Here we are." Dad steered starboard into the empty lot behind Don's Last Stand and parked.

"What are we doing here?" I asked. "We just ate."

151

"Don was with the Drug Enforcement Agency," Dad said "He busted the stoner hippies that used to own this joint. Then he bought it in a government auction and retired. Don still has a lot of contacts."

"How do you know all that stuff?"

"Guys tell more things to their mechanics than they tell their wives or even their bartenders," Dad said. "I figure Don can get that film of yours developed without every Bob, John, and Colonel Sanders knowing about it."

"Makes sense," I said. "I guess."

We got out of the bus. I remembered last night's dream. "Do you think Tom McCall is behind this?" I asked. "Do you think he wants my film?"

Dad stopped dead in his tracks and his face turned red. "I'm going to pretend I didn't hear that, Junior." The last time I saw Dad get that mad was when I asked him why people laugh at the phrase "snug harbor."

"Sorry," I said.

Don's back door looked to be made out of blast proof, reinforced metal – as if he was preparing for an armed invasion.

"He's expecting us." I thought Dad was going to perform some kind of secret knock, or something, but he just yelled. "Hey, Don! Open up!"

The door opened just a half-inch, and Don peeked out. "Is it just the two of you?"

"Affirmative," Dad said.

"And you have the football?"

Football? Then I realized that Don was referring to my film.

"Affirmative," Dad said.

"Ten four," I said. CB lingo was very popular at

the time, good buddy.

Don pushed the door open. I followed Dad inside.

The air smelled of gun oil. There were cinder block walls without windows. Filtered air vents. Short wave radio equipment. Maps. And African violets, blooming under artificial light.

Don caught me looking. "I grow African violets. So what?"

"Nothing." I said. "Nothing at all."

"They help me relax," Don said. "Let's have the football."

I looked to Dad. He nodded that it was OK, so I gave my film cans to Don.

"I have a contact at Elmendorf," Don said. "After this material is processed, I will deliver it back to you in person. There will be no written orders or receipts, no paper trail of any kind. This is a dark phantom operation. Are we clear?"

Before Dad and I could think of a cool *Mission Impossible* way to say yes, there was a crashing sound: Metal, clanging on a tile floor. Then, a seething, hellish hiss, like a dozen oysters, all wet and fresh out of the shell, being plunged into a deep fat fryer. Wild yelling.

Those yells got louder, more frantic, and turned into a long roar of pain and anger. I recognized Ronny's voice.

Don's eyes got wide. He turned and ran to the kitchen. Dad and I ran after him. We found Ronny, lying on the kitchen floor. There was a deep, stainless steel pan on the floor next to him. That pan had contained sizzling-hot cooking oil until just a few seconds ago, but now it was empty. Apparently, Ronny had been carrying the pan, and then dropped it. That hot oil had spilled onto Ronny's legs and thighs. The whole kitchen smelled of oil and of something burning, cooking.

Don and Dad pulled Ronny's arms and dragged him toward the sink at the other side of the kitchen. They took off Ronny's shoes and loosened his belt and pulled off his blue jeans.

Ronny yelled and growled, again and again. I put my hands over my ears, but I could still hear him. I didn't want to see what the hot oil had done to Ronny's legs, but I saw. His bare skin was red and raw and blistered in places. I closed my eyes as tight as I could and tried to think of something else, anything else. Dinosaurs. Monsters. Medieval dragons. Disney's re-animated brain, even. But nothing worked.

"Call an ambulance, Junior." Dad's voice was firm and even.

I opened my eyes. Don pointed to a wall phone. I slipped in the oil a little as I ran to it. My hands were shaking as I picked up the receiver and dialed zero for the operator. Ronny kept yelling and the operator couldn't hear me so I had to shout into the phone. I didn't know the address, but the operator knew where Don's Last Stand was and she told me that an ambulance was on the way.

Don soaked some towels in cold water. Dad held Ronny down as Don covered Ronny's lower body and legs with the wet towels. Don's hands were trembling, and he was actually crying. Dad just frowned and sweated, and he was breathing hard.

I hung up the phone. My own hands were shaking. I was scared and mad, so I ran out of there as fast as I could and back out to the bus. I climbed up into the front seat and stared out the windshield – at a small group of Pterosaurs, drying their damp, translucent wings in the weak spring sunlight and snapping at each other with voices that sounded like the buzz and clank of cheap windup toys.

The Pterosaurs had skeletal faces, and when their beaks were closed, their tiny stained teeth stuck out at odd angles.

*"They were the lowly airborne vermin of the prehistoric world!"*

I wanted to kill them, stomp them, shoot them, pick them off one at a time and do them all a favor. I quick bullet to the skull would be better than a short life as an infested, infected scavenger, fated to be swallowed whole by a predator or pecked to death and then eaten by your own hideous kind. So I pointed my gun finger at each of the Pterosaurs, fired, and watched them fly apart, disintegrate, one after the other, until they were all dead and in broken, twitching pieces. But I didn't feel any better. If anything, I felt worse. I felt guilty.

I wanted Pam Grier to show up and tell me that everything was going to be OK. But Julie appeared instead, looking just the way she had looked down on the beach the other morning, and she was careful not to step on the dead Pterosaur parts. As she walked up to the bus in slow motion, I could tell she had something to say, something that would make me feel better. But then the ambulance arrived, siren blaring, and Julie went away like sand in the wind.

A few minutes later, the paramedics brought Ronny out on a stretcher. He was quiet now, and his face was white, and I thought he was probably in a state of shock. As the paramedics loaded Ronny into the back of the ambulance, he stared right at me, as if this was all my fault, somehow. Was he right? Had I caused this to happen?

It seemed like a long time before Dad came out to

the bus and got in. I might have fallen asleep for a while. Dad had cooking oil on his shirt and pants, and he smelled like oil, too. "You OK, Junior?"

"Yeah." My voice broke a little because I was trying not to cry.

I guess Dad could tell, because, without any kind of set up, he told me a story that I hadn't heard before.

"It was the spring of 1962. We were two days out of Subic Bay, the Philippines. It was a clear morning, and a great day to be a sailor. I was on the quarterdeck that morning, drinking coffee and staring out over the water. Our Filipino cook made the best coffee, Junior. It was always strong and thick and never seemed to get cold.

I had just come off duty, had just finished chow, and was looking forward to some sack time. But someone had to ruin things. Just had to. You know how it goes.

Ensign Robert J. Bullock, a four-masted jerk-spoon if ever there was one, started slappin' a ration on me, chewin' me out for something or another. I can't even remember why. Maybe it was because I had taken a precious three-bounce cup from his mess hall without permission. Maybe he knew I was a surfer. Maybe he didn't even have a reason. Bullock was like that."

Ensign Bullock sounded like the kind of guy that would throw an orange at you, give you a black eye, or maybe choke you in your own bed.

"All I could do was stand at attention, take his grief, and then salute. Of course, in my mind, I was tapping his birdy head with a pipe wrench the whole time. Tap. Tap. Tap. And then, just as Bullock turned

156

to leave and go ruin someone else's day, I shot him the finger. But I guess I was sleepy or just plain slow because he caught me.

Now remember, it was a clear, cloudless day, so I can't explain what happened next. The Navy said it was a waterspout, or maybe a typhoon. I can't imagine how the C.O. wrote it up later. Killed In Action, I'll bet, since Bullock was an officer, and all. But for whatever unfathomable, unexplainable, seemingly random-but-I-know-better reason, a six-hundred-pound grand piano came spinning down out of that perfect Pacific sky, landed right on top of Ensign Bullock, and squashed him like an earwig. Missed me by three feet, max.

As long as I live, I'll never forget that sound. It was like a musical bomb. Piano keys and wires and wood and jerk-face, all smashing together at the same time."

Why was Dad telling this story?

"Karma, Junior. Retribution. Wheel in the Sky. What goes around comes around. This wasn't your fault."

"My fault?" How was this my fault?

"Ronny chose to be a bilge-boot. Bad stuff happens to bilge-boots. Eventually."

Did Ronny get burned because of something I'd done?

"Let's go home," Dad said. I watched as he turned the key in the ignition and started the engine. His hand was strong and it didn't shake at all. When we pulled out of the parking lot, we ran right over the dead bodies of those nasty Pterosaurs.

We didn't listen to the radio or Dad's eight track player and we didn't say anything to each other. I just wanted to go to bed and fall into a deep sleep and not dream about anything at all.

On the way back to our house on Desdemona Street, Dad picked up a six pack of Oly. When we got home, Dad cracked one of the beers, and put the rest in the reefer. Then he sat down at the kitchen table with Ma, sipped his beer, and filled her in on all the details.

I went upstairs and sat down outside Stephanie's door. "Hey, Steph. It's me."

Maybe I was just tired, or maybe I was in some type of shock, myself. But at that moment, I knew that Stephanie was sitting on the other side of the door and listening to my every word and nodding her head and being very nice about it. I just knew it.

"I didn't want anybody to get hurt," I said. "If this is Karma, then I don't want any part of it, you know what I mean?"

Steph understood. I could tell. And it felt so good to know that she was on my side. "They're going to blow up Mister Fishback's Monster at nine o'clock on Saturday morning," I said. "Nobody knows what it is or where it came from, but they're going to blow it up with TNT. Isn't that crazy?"

I thought I heard Steph answer, say something.

"What did you say?" I put my hand on the doorknob, gave it a half-turn, and was about to go inside. "Stephanie?"

But as I listened, all I heard was the Grim Reaper from *Senior Skip Day*, laughing and cackling, and I realized that of course Steph was dead and that I would never see her again and that life was just an endless driver's ed film – one tragic and ugly scene after another.

I didn't go in. I still wasn't ready.

Not yet.

I went on to my room and threaded up *The Cyclops Escapes*. It was my first ever flick, and you could sure tell. The animation was jerky, and you could see my fingerprints in the clay.

The Cyclops was the same one that Ronny had smashed. I remembered making it. And putting wooden dowels inside the legs to keep it standing up straight.

# Chapter Twenty-Three

## Friday

I didn't want to remember how Ronny had been so terribly burned, or imagine the pain he must have felt, or even think about what had happened at all. I just wanted to edit that entire scene right out of the movie and leave it on the cutting room floor.

Some people – like Ma – can put ugly things out of their heads. And for good. It's easy for them. They just don't think about whatever is bothering them, and then move on to something else.

But that kind of thing was never easy for me. I tried to replace the thoughts that I didn't want with other thoughts, scenes from other movies. But sometimes those pictures and noises were even worse. When that happened, the best thing for me to do was make something.

So I got up early that morning and went out to Dad's shop to make some baby Tyrannosaurs. *Epoch Lost* was going to end with an entire litter of the little carnivores, playing like puppies in the ruins of Seaport City Hall – after mankind has nuked or polluted or just plain dumbed itself out of existence, thereby allowing evolution to start all over again. I thought the film school snobs would like that kind of cynical,

160

downbeat ending.

I sat down at my workbench and grabbed that wad of cold, gray-green clay that had been a Brachiosaurus just a few days ago, and tore a big handful out of it. Then I punched it down, rolled it out, and folded it over again and again and again. When it was pliable, I added some yellow clay to lighten the color and started rolling and folding all over again.

My knuckles cracked. My palms ached a little. But it felt good.

"You OK, Junior?" Dad was working on his side of the shop.

I wondered how long he'd been over there. "Yep."

"You let me know if you want to talk, OK?"

"OK, Dad."

Dad didn't say anything else. I didn't start a conversation. I guess we were both trying to get yesterday out of our heads, each in our own way, by making, building. Creating.

I started knuckling, poking, and crab-clawing the clay into shape, forming two Theropod bodies with heads and tails, and then detailing two tiny snarly faces. Little by little, I began to feel better. More relaxed. Calm. I knew that I was the only one on the entire planet that was making a set of baby Tyrannosaurs, and those toothy siblings were all that mattered right now.

Legs. Forearms. Eyes. At the end of two hours, I had two T. Rex babies, each about four inches high. Twins, just like Stephanie and me. I wondered, what would Ms. Ellerath think about that? But for some reason, one of the twins looked meaner, nastier than the other. Why? What was the symbolism? For a second, I freaked a little and thought maybe I should smash them both, just like Ronny had smashed my

Cyclops, and then start all over again. But then I decided to quit for the day.

I hadn't forgotten about Ronny, but I had stopped dwelling on what had happened to him, and that was good enough for now. I put the Rex twins on the window sill to chill. They sure looked cute together.

Later that morning, I called Ken and told him all about my getting choked the night before.

He didn't take the news very well. "Are you OK? Are you sure? Did you get X-rays? Are the cops going to put you in protective custody? No? Why not? I'll go get Mihn so we can pull a stake out at your house tonight!"

"Don't worry about me," I said. "I've got Ma for protection." Then I told Ken about Ronny getting hurt.

"Rough justice." I heard Ken banging on a wall or a table or something with each infuriated syllable. "That creep got what he deserved! He's been asking for it!"

"I'm not so sure." Then I heard scratching and rapid fire chattering on the other end of the line. "How's Zombie's eye?"

"Spinning like a lopsided top," Ken said. "He can hear your voice."

"I love that sorry beast."

"Me, too," Ken said. "Kinda. Do you want to do anything today?"

"I think I'll just stay home," I said. "I still have that dumb paper to write for Ms. Ellerath." That would be another project to keep my head occupied.

"OK. Let me know if you change your mind."

"Thanks, Ken."

"Roger."

Then I called Mihn, went through the usual telephone preliminaries, and filled him in on the Martian attack and Ronny's injury.

"Maybe we should go visit Ronny in the hospital," he said.

"Maybe," I said, even though I really didn't want to do that. "Maybe later."

"Do you want to go to Don's to eat and laugh at tourist asses?"

"I don't think I'll be going back to Don's anytime soon."

"I understand," Mihn said, and he changed the subject. "Have you seen the newspaper this morning?

"No. Why?"

"The scientists at OSU say they know what that thing on the beach actually is. Do you want me to tell you, or do you want to read the ass for yourself?"

I saw a copy of the local paper on the kitchen table. "I'll check it out myself. Thanks, though."

"OK," Mihn said. "Well, good bye, Steve."

"Good bye, Mihn." I hung up, sat down at the table, and flipped through the pages of *The Seaport Semaphore*. Sure enough, toward the back of the paper, where nobody would see it, was the story, "MONSTER" EXPLAINED.

According to OSU, The Monster was nothing more than a, "massive tangle of marine debris, both organic and manmade, that had been trapped in the currents that converge and swirl between Asia and North America, and then released by a recent storm to wash up in Seaport."

In other words, Mister Fishback's Monster wasn't some Indian omen, or the byproduct of a covert government operation, or an undiscovered species, or the last living remnant of the Mesozoic Age. It was just something that the mighty Pacific Ocean had coughed up in the same undignified way that a cat coughs up an annoying hairball. But bigger. The story also detailed the when and where of the upcoming detonation.

So, no big deal. Move along, folks, there's nothing to see here. Go on home so we can blow the thing up and turn it into free lunch for every scavenger and bottom feeder on the West Coast and then move on with the rest of our lives.

Kind of a letdown, as far as I was concerned. And totally undignified. I wasn't about to be part of the cheesy sendoff of Mister Fishback's Monster. It just didn't feel right to me. If Ken and Mihn wanted to go, that was their business.

But then I started thinkin'. The great Kong had died a noble, Shakespearean death – falling, shot and broken-hearted, from the very top of the world after losing Fay Wray. Everybody remembers that scene, and not just special effects nerds like me, because everyone felt bad for the old boy. That's how all the great monsters met their end, with all the tragic, epic spectacle of a Norse saga. Frankenstein. The Wolf Man. The Phantom of the Opera. Godzilla, even.

And they all taught us a lesson about our own arrogance and fear of things we don't understand.

But Mister Fishback's Monster wouldn't be allowed that kind of dramatic, memorable demise. And there would be no lesson, either. Sure, there would be a spectacular explosion, but then, just a smoking hole in the sand, a bad smell on the wind – and a sense of relief. Our Monster was nothing more than an unsightly, smelly nuisance. Yesterday's news.

But as far as I was concerned, my mysterious gassy

friend still had something to teach us. He deserved to be immortalized, not just flushed back out to sea like a colossal turd.

And I knew three guys and a freaky-looking ferret that were up to the challenge.

# Chapter Twenty-Four

## Saturday Morning

Another nice day on Ono Beach. It was almost nine o'clock – Zero Hour. Mister Fishback's Monster was about to be blown up, atomized, and turned into fish food. It seemed like half the known world had come to see the big kiss off. And then celebrate. The whole thing still felt sleazy to me, exploitative. Just plain wrong.

But I had made a solemn pledge to every poor, misunderstood creature that had ever been chased by an angry mob of torch-bearing Hollywood extras, or cornered in some dank studio sewer, or pursued to the top of a national monument: I would honor The Monster's end – and on film, even though I still wasn't how to pull it off. He deserved that much after all the staring and the guessing and the stupid pranks.

Unfortunately, Ono Beach was under martial law. The beach itself and all the access roads had been blocked off, and were being guarded by military police troops. Big guys with guns. Anyone that wanted to see the explosion – or preserve the event on Kodachrome, like me – had to do so from the relative safety of the parking lot above the beach.

Ken parked the T-Bird in the high beach grass because there were no parking spaces left. "You

166

should be able to get a good view from up here."

The Monster, roped off and surrounded by soldiers wearing gas masks, looked flat this morning. Pathetic. It was as if someone had pulled the plug on one of those big parade balloons. The hide was starting to split in places, revealing rotten muscle and white bone underneath. You could see dynamite sticks, taped together and stuffed up under the leeward side of the thing. Sea gulls were already going to town. That putrid stink was still heavy in the air.

"Look at all the cameras," Mihn said. "Hundreds of them!"

He was right. Everybody seemed to have an Instamatic or a Brownie, loaded and ready for action. I saw a man with a super eight movie camera, and I was a little jealous.

"That's the problem," I said. "When the Hindenburg exploded in 1937, a hundred reporters took the exact same picture at the exact same moment, and to this day, that's the only image that people remember. That's why I want something different. My shot has to be better, more spectacular, and more memorable than anyone else's."

Ken had a few ideas. "3D? Sensorama? Smell-O-Vision?"

"Give me a break." I was starting to get arty-cranky, like some teenage Otto Preminger, or something.

"In every American movie I have ever seen," Mihn said, "the explosions are always in slow motion."

"Slow motion?" Ken asked. "Slow motion! Can you do that, Steve?"

"Yes." I sat up. "I sure can!"

Zombie's ears went back and his tongue flicked in

and out.

"You can't do better than a slow motion explosion," Ken said. "Ka-boosh!"

"OK." I set the frames per second to 48. "This just might work after all!"

The three of us got out of the T-Bird. Zombie stayed in the car because Ken thought the blast would scare the poor mutt to death. We maneuvered our way through the crowd and to the edge of the parking lot. I had never seen so many people all together in one place. Locals. Tourists. Kids. Grownups. People from other countries, even.

*"The yapping throng had come from around the world to witness the epic end of terror!"*

"Ooh," Ken said. "Brownies!"

Sure enough. Crazy Annie was there, too, dressed in black, working the crowd, and peddling her fudge and who-knows-what-else brownies.

"Easy, Ken," Mihn said.

No sign of Julie Smith. Probably just as well. But I saw Mister Trammell, pink and peeling, preaching to a small group of Asian folks. I couldn't hear what he was saying, but his audience seemed to be hanging on his every crazy, probably inebriated word.

Time was slipping away. I needed to set up. There was a sandy rise at the edge of the lot that looked like it would give me a good view of the beach below – a master shot. "Ken," I said, "see if you can find a chunk of driftwood, something warped and gnarled."

"Can do." Without asking why, Ken started the search.

Mihn stood at attention, awaiting orders.

"Follow me," I said.

Mihn saluted. "Yes, sir!"

We jogged over to the rise. I kneeled in the sand, aimed my camera down at The Monster, and peered into the view finder with my almost healed eye. "Boring," I said. "Boring!"

Ken joined us. He had a three-foot length of twisty, sun-bleached driftwood. "Will his do?" he asked. "It looks like an alien *hara-kiri* knife."

"Perfect!" I jammed the driftwood into the sand in front of me, tilted it just a little, and checked my viewfinder again. Now I had a cool angle: The Monster at the center of the shot, half-framed in one corner by driftwood – which, because it was so close to the lens, would be slightly out of focus. "I'm ready!"

There was a loud blast of an air horn, followed by a piercing shriek of feedback. Down below, sea gulls took to the air, and soldiers jumped into jeeps and split for safety. Behind us and off to our left, an Army corporal stood up in the back of a jeep and addressed the attendees through an olive drab megaphone: "Good morning, ladies and gentlemen." More feedback. "We will now begin our countdown."

The crowd grew silent. All you could hear were the waves and the wind.

The corporal looked at his watch. He waited. And then he began. "Thirty seconds . . ."

Dads hoisted their kids up onto their shoulders. Moms pointed. A man put on a pair of sunglasses, and I had to wonder what he was expecting. An atomic flash, maybe?

"Ten seconds . . ."

Two images came to mind almost simultaneously. One was the little girl in that famous black and white political commercial from the late sixties, plucking pedals from a daisy and counting to herself – as the

169

sky above her erupts with radioactive fire. And I thought of The Monster itself, just an innocent victim of whatever weird oceanographic circumstance, cast ashore to be freak-gawked, and about to be blown into a million tiny pieces of blubber and bone and all the other things that monsters are made of.

No matter what it actually was, Mister Fishback's Monster was just one more misunderstood misfit in a long line of monsters, mutants, and freaks. All of them had been ridiculed, chased, mobbed, misjudged, and finally, condemned. And they had all been friends of mine. I suddenly found myself feeling very sad.

"Good bye, Mister Monster," Mihn said. "It was nice to know you."

Ken sang a line from a song by The Doors: "This is the end, beautiful friend."

"Five, four . . ."

Action! I started shooting. The camera whirred as film flew from the top reel, through the gate, and onto the take-up reel. Forty-eight frames per second, more than twice the normal speed.

"Three, two, one . . ."

But there was no explosion. Instead, that air horn blared over and over again. Sirens whined at a high pitch. Folks yelled. It was like the Russians were attacking, or something.

Cut!" I turned to my friends. "What's going on?"

Ken pointed. "Look, it's Fishback!"

Sure enough, Mister Fishback was down on the beach – being chased by three military police soldiers. Our teacher's sore, smashed foot had apparently mended, because he was faster than any of the MPs. On the other hand, those MP's had .45 caliber pistols and night sticks and they didn't necessarily need a lot of speed or agility.

"What's he doing?" Mihn asked. "Is he crazy?"

Mister Fishback ran clockwise around his Monster, almost lapping the MP's, and all the while shouting something up to all of us. I couldn't hear him, but people up in the parking lot laughed and applauded. It seemed like everybody was on Fishback's side.

One of the soldiers got the bright idea to stop, go the other way around, and trap Mister F. But when Fishback saw that he was about to be caught, he jumped up onto The Monster and actually started climbing it.

A deafening roar went up. Whistles and cheers. It was as if The Mighty Casey hadn't struck out, after all.

But Mister Fishback didn't get very far. The MP's grabbed him by the cuffs of his pants and pulled him down to the sand.

"That's not right!" Ken had that look in his eye again – just like when I got hit in the face by that orange just a little over a week ago. I could tell he wanted to charge down to the beach, trash a few soldiers, and then rescue Mister Fishback. He actually growled.

"Easy," I said. "Those guys have guns."

"Guns," Mihn said.

The MP's slapped handcuffs on him and dragged him out of sight. I distinctly heard Crazy Annie yell out, "Make brownies, not war!"

"What will happen to Mister Fishback?" Mihn asked "Will he be arrested? Will he be fired for this?"

I turned to answer, and something behind Mihn caught my eye: It was that black Cadillac again, cruising slowly through the parking lot as if looking for someone.

171

*"It was a dark and gleaming, four-wheeled symbol of doom!"*

"I hope he'll be OK," I said.

"He is a good teacher," Mihn said.

"The best," Ken said.

A minute or so later, the corporal started the countdown a second time. I forgot about the mysterious black Caddy – for the time being. It was time to get back to work.

I squinted through the viewfinder and held my breath. This time, there were no last minute interruptions.

Action! I held my camera tight and braced for an epic blast. But there wasn't one. There was an explosion, and it made my ears ring, but it wasn't very spectacular at all. Mister Fishback's Monster just went away, that's all. No fiery flash. No thunderous blast. No ominous mushroom cloud. It was like a disappointing magic trick. Now you see it, now you don't.

Cut! I hoped the blast would look better in slow motion. Behind me, people hooted and applauded as if watching fireworks on the Fourth of July.

*"The terrible sea demon had been banished, sent back to the foaming sea from whence he came!"*

I set the film speed back to the usual setting.

"There," Ken said. "Show's over, buddy." But the show wasn't over. It had only just started.

Now, everybody knows that it rains a lot in Oregon, especially on the Coast. Most folks that live here are used to the rain. We even like it. Rain can be calming, cleansing. Refreshing. But that day, as we all stood, post-explosion, there above the beach, the rain wasn't refreshing at all. It was sticky and rotten and it

172

smelled terrible.

This time, the rain was blood – old, dead and semi-clotted blood – hissing down out of a clear blue sky.

Confusion. Uncertainty. Even laughter. What in the world? People in the crowd actually looked up.

Then, chunks. Hunks. Wet things. Bits and pieces of Mister Fishback's Monster. Meat. Guts. Unidentified rotten, rubbery stuff. Parts. Pieces. Assorted, miscellaneous putridity. It all came showering down.

Action! Something the size of a soccer ball, something that looked like a big wet scab, landed on top of some poor lady's head and plastered her hair down. When the little kid standing with the lady looked up to see what Mommy was screaming about, something long-dead and spongy fell right into his open mouth.

I kept shooting. Falling gristle. Blubber. Corruption. Chaos. It was as if a bomb had gone off in that huge fish market in Tokyo.

A suction cup, flapping like a bat as it fell, hit an old man in the back of the neck and knocked him to the ground.

Nobody was spared – including me. I could feel tiny wet pieces of The Monster land, cold and sticky, on the back of my neck and on my arms.

Screams of panic and disgust. People started scrambling for the safety of their cars.

"Let's beat it!" Ken grabbed Mihn and me by the arms and yanked hard. "We'll be killed!"

"This is terrible!" Mihn said. "Terrible ass!"

But I loved every blood-basted second of this movie.

On the way to the T-Bird, we passed Mister

Trammell, standing with his hands in the air and cackling like a crazy man. "I warned you!" he shrieked. "I warned you all!" His bald head and face were besmeared with dead foulness. This was the rain of bitter vengeance that the old man had so ominously foretold.

I caught it all on the run, hoping I wouldn't run out of film. When we got to Ken's T-Bird, Ken threw me in the back seat, and then Mihn in front.

Cut! We were safe. Zombie, whining and shaking and obviously freaked out by all the chaos, came out from under the front seat. He bounced from Ken's shoulder to Mihn's and then to mine. I tried to comfort the poor beast. "It's OK, Zomb. It's just a dead monster gut storm."

Ken squinted through the grue-spotted windshield to the carnage outside. "I can't believe it! It happened exactly like that old coot said it would!" Then he saw his own reflection in the rear view mirror – and all the clotted blood and sand and who-knows-what-else on his face. "Gross!" He looked at Mihn, then me. "We look like we've been in a car wreck!"

"Ass!" Mihn realized that he was likewise streaked and smeared with deceased monster residue, and started checking himself for injuries.

I decided to mess with him a little. "Maybe we're dead," I said, "and we don't know it yet!" I think I got that idea from an old episode of *The Twilight Zone*. Maybe it was *Night Gallery*.

"That's not funny!" But when Mihn realized that he was intact and breathing, he started laughing – Mihn style.

I wasn't hurt, but I was afraid that Ma was going to snap an axle when she saw how filthy I was, and I wondered if either Ken's grandmother or Mihn's mom could wash my clothes before I went home.

Outside, things had calmed down. The gut shower had ended, at least. We got out of the car – with Zombie clinging to my neck for dear life – and I started firing off some pick-up shots. Inserts. Details. Blood. Organs. Car damage. Ken's white and bloody T-Bird. Army jeeps and trucks. And I grabbed a killer shot of the BEACH ACCESS sign, dripping with dead, wet yucky.

With only one or two feet of film left, I got the four of us in a huddle, held the camera at arm's length, and filmed us in all our post-explosion nastiness. Three filthy, blood-and-gut-spattered faces, three big smiles, and a pop-eyed, bald-headed ferret.

Years later, I blew up a frame of that shot and framed it as a souvenir of our adventure, and of our friendship.

I was out of film by then, but I knew that I had some great images for my flick. Looking back, though, I wish I had brought along an extra roll so I would have a record of what happened next.

Just as Ken cranked the ignition, the dark shadow of a man started tapping on Mihn's red-smeared window.

"Be careful," I said.

"Maybe he's hurt." Mihn rolled down the window.

"Mornin' fellas." Mister Fishback spoke in a quiet voice, and he was not decorated with blood and tiny pieces of monster.

"Are you a fugitive?" Mihn asked. "A refugee?"

"You could say that," Mister Fishback said, and now I noticed the sand in his hair and jaw-beard, the cut on his lower lip. And the handcuffs. He looked beat up and desperate. "Can I catch a ride with you?"

175

"Get in," Ken said. "We saw what those jerk weeds did to you back there."

Mihn climbed into the back with Zombie and me. Mister Fishback took shotgun and ducked down out of sight.

"How did you get away?" I asked.

"Those soldiers are in good shape," Mister Fishback said, "but they're not long distance runners."

"Won't they be looking for you?" I asked.

Mister Fishback laughed. "I wasn't carrying any ID. It's a trick I learned in the sixties."

"Let's scram." Ken steered the great white Thunderbird out of the grass and back onto the black top. Only a few people had come to their senses after the big monster shower, and they were either sitting in their cars or trying to take in a little fresh air, so there was no log jam of cars trying to get out of the parking lot and onto the Coast Highway,

But just when it looked like we'd survived, just when it looked like we were all going to get out of there, safe and relatively unscathed, I saw that black Cadillac again, bloody, now, and just twenty feet away.

Looking back on that day, I think maybe I should've minded my own business, because when I told Ken, "There it is, the getaway car for whoever it was that choked me, and tried to steal my film," he got that loony look on his face again, and asked if I was sure. And when I checked more closely and saw a hundred tiny dents in the Caddy – of the type made by shotgun BB's – and said, "Yes, I'm sure," Ken stomped on the gas without a moment's hesitation, roared like a bull Sasquatch, and rammed his white Thunderbird right into the driver's side of the black Cadillac.

Ka-runch! Buckled metal. Shattered window glass. Gushing radiator fluid. Flying ferret. It was a scene right out of one of Mister Kaufman's driver's ed movies. But real, and not as sad.

Then everything stopped. Ken bailed out of his crashed T-Bird, crawled up onto the hood of the black Caddy, and started banging on the windshield and roof. "Come out of there and face justice, you tint-glass cowards!"

As Ken wailed away on the Cadillac, a freaked out, over-stimulated Zombie leaped up onto Mister Fishback's head and proceeded to mate with the science teacher's ear.

I won't go into descriptive details.

"Hey!" Mister Fishback was much calmer than I would've been if a ferret had tried to make love to my ear. He just grabbed Zombie by the scruff of the neck, peeled him away, and then held him suspended in midair. Not an easy move if you're wearing handcuffs.

The rest of us crawled out of the dented Thunderbird.

"Nobody strangles one of my buddies and gets away with it!" Ken started yanking on the driver's side door and actually banging his head against the tinted window. Good thing he's on our side, I thought.

We heard a muffled voice from inside the Caddy. "OK, OK, we're coming out!"

Ken backed off – just a little. "You've got two seconds!"

The same muffled voice: "We'll have to use the passenger door!"

"Fine with me!" Ken went around to the other side of the car. "I can kick ass on either side!"

I didn't want anybody to get hurt – not even the Martian strangler. "Don't hurt 'em, Ken!" More than

177

anything else, I just wanted to know who was inside the Caddy.

"Come on out," Mister Fishback said, still hoisting an amorous ferret – and watching out for soldiers.

And then two men emerged from the crunched Cadillac. The first man was the same height and weight of the Martian that had choked me. And he wore blue, mechanic's coveralls. But I wasn't totally sure if it was the same guy.

The second man was none other than Mister Les Schwab, multimillionaire tire mogul and television personality. At the moment, he wasn't wearing his famous cowboy hat, and I had to wonder if he had sent it to the cleaners after vomiting into it.

We all backed away. Ken included. It was a reflex. We had been conditioned by all those commercials. Les Schwab was an Oregon icon, a rugged, hardworking, honest and trustworthy man – kind of like Tom McCall, but with tires.

Ken was the first to snap out of it. He pointed to the guy in coveralls – the mechanic. "Is this the low life thug that tried to strangle you, Steve?"

"Maybe." I was pretty sure the guy was the Martian, but I knew that if I said so, Ken would probably beat the poor dude to within an inch of his life. "Maybe not."

Mister Schwab turned to the mechanic. "Did you lay a hand on this young Oregonian?"

"He had the film," the mechanic said, and now I recognized the voice. He was the Martian, after all. No doubt about it.

"Film?" Mister Schwab shook his head in disgust. "If you weren't my son-in-law . . ."

At that, Ken ran at the mechanic – arms spread

178

wide, taped fingers curled and ready to wrap themselves around a windpipe. Mihn, Mister Fishback – still holding a visibly aroused Zombie – and I did our best to block Ken, but he still managed to connect a solid punch to the man's jaw.

The mechanic, the former Martian strangler, went down. Hard, too. I actually felt bad for him.

"Mother of pearl!" Ken had hurt his hand again.

"Mister Schwab?" I had to know. "Why did you want my film?"

"I didn't want it. Mister Schwab let his man lay unattended. "But the company that does my commercials said that if pictures of me throwing up into my hat ever got out, they would ruin my image, and put me in the poor house."

"I can see that." Now, I understood. The whole thing made sense. I looked over the scene: two wrecked cars, a guy laying on his face, a famous millionaire, and a science teacher wearing handcuffs and holding a horny ferret. "So what happens now?"

Mister Schwab smiled, just like in his commercials and on his bill boards. "Let's talk."

"What's there to talk about?" Ken was still steamed.

"Your silence," Mister Schwab said. "And your promise that you won't sell that vomit film to anybody. I'm sure we can all come to some financial understanding."

179

# Chapter Twenty Five

## Easter Sunday Morning

"I truly believe that I could eat nothing but fried smelt for the rest of my life," Dad said.

"I concur." Ken sat back and made his chair creak.

"Me, too," I said.

"Me, three." Ma picked up our plates and silverware and took them to her avocado kitchen.

What are smelt? They are fish, about four inches long. In 1806, the chief of the Clatsop tribe introduced smelt to Lewis and Clark. Mister Lewis then praised the fish in his historic journal: "I think them superior to any fish I ever tasted."

How do you cook smelt? You ask your Ma to dust a few dozen of the fish with flour and black pepper and then fry them up whole, just like we did every year on Easter. Then, after stuffing ourselves, we always went down to The Pier for the blessing of the fishing fleet. That was how we celebrated the holiday in my family: little fried fish, and then prayers for safety and a good haul. No dyed eggs or plastic grass or jelly beans for us.

And what better way to draw the curtain on such a weird and exciting week of bullies and monsters and raining guts? I had invited Ken and Mihn, of course. Ken came, but Mihn and his family would be on their fishing boat today, receiving the benediction.

Ken produced a brown rectangle of flat, dried meat. "May I offer you gentlemen some antelope jerky from Eastern Oregon?"

"Don't mind if I do," Dad said.

"No pepperoni?" I asked.

"This is a special occasion." Ken tore off a piece of jerky with freshly re-taped fingers, and passed it around.

After breakfast we all left our house on Desdemona Street and walked down to the sea. The cool spring mist was so light that it didn't soak into our clothes or our hair. It just felt cool and clean — and without any blood and guts. The mist had burned off by the time we got to The Pier, where we all stood at the railing — along with almost every other non-fishing family in town — and waited for the service to start.

Below us, boats were neat in their slips. Captains and crews and families all stood on deck. Not exactly church-going types, most of them, not on most days, at least. Tattooed arms. Bleary eyes and bloated faces. Overalls. Boots and gloves. But today, those folks all looked humble and gentle and grateful.

"There's Mihn." Ken pointed.

Mihn stood with his parents on the deck of their charter boat, *Trang Chủ*. Mihn looked a lot like his mom. Mihn's dad looked strong, but his face looked worn.

"Where's Mai?" Ken asked.

Fishing widows and their kids sat together under a black canvas awning. I was surprised by how young most of the women were. Young or old, all of them looked injured, weary, but strong at the same time. Unbowed. Unbeaten. They had lost their men to the

181

sea, and now they were here at the edge of the very water that had taken their husbands away, to pray for the safety of other fishing families.

A priest sat with the widows. Father Kevin, the head priest at Saint Mary's by the Sea, looked to be in his fifties. He was bald with a long white beard that made him look like either an extra in a Cecil B. DeMille movie, or a member of the band ZZ Top.

I had met Father Kevin on the morning we buried Steph. Later on that same day, I sat on the front porch of our house on Desdemona Street, staring up into a white, drizzling sky, trying to forget about things and probably imagining some weird scene or another. I guess after a while I got bored, though, and decided to go inside. When I opened the front door, Father Kevin, dressed all in black, was there in the entryway, about to leave. His beard was shorter then. He put his warm hands to the sides of my cold face and it felt good.

Ma thought Father Kevin was a holy man. I just thought he was a cool guy.

And then the ceremony started. Father Kevin wore a white robe made of course cloth, and a small wooden cross hanging from a string around his neck. He rowed a small wooden boat out to the middle of the harbor so that he was surrounded on three sides by the fishing boats and families of Sea Port. Behind him, Lindsey Bay, and then the open sea, which was calm today.

Father Kevin stood up in his row boat, sure and steady. He raised his hands above his head and closed his eyes. Then he spoke in a clear, booming voice.

"Your only son chose fishermen, not kings nor scholars nor even clerics, to join him and preach to

182

the world. He chose men with net-scarred hands and strong sea legs, He called you fishermen, to be his disciples.

When Jesus wanted to teach us about faith, he stepped out of a fishing boat, walked upon the very sea, and then asked us to follow him. He fed the multitude, not with meat or fowl, but with fish, and simple loaves of bread. And historians tell us that the outline of a fish was the first symbol of the Christian church, before it was replaced by the image of the bloody cross.

But life at sea is a hard life. We see these women, left without husbands, these children left without fathers. And we live in constant fear of that phone call in the middle of the night. But despite the danger, we climb into our boats every morning and take once again to the sea. Why?"

I remembered how Mihn's family had taken to the sea, after Saigon fell. I thought about their harrowing escape, and about how Mihn seemed to be a very happy person that, as far as I knew, didn't need anything thing like Steve-O-Scope to escape from the real world. Why?

When I looked over to *Trang Chủ*, I saw Mihn and Mai standing close together, now, both listening intently to the service. Then Mihn kissed Mai on the cheek – and held it.

"Did you see that?" Ken asked.

"Why?" Father Kevin went on. "Because these women and young ones know, just as we all know, that there is no light without the dark, no sweet without the bitter, and in order to know love, we must also risk the searing, hellish pain of loss and of loneliness. But we, all of us, choose to love, anyway, and we choose faith, anyway. We choose. We choose, and we gather again this year to ask not only for safe seas and full nets, but also for the courage to color our lives with faith and hope, not fear and bitterness.

This is a lesson that our souls must learn. And it is a hard lesson. Our lives are but a prelude, a coming attraction, for something greater."

Coming attraction? Was Father Kevin a movie fan?

"Let us pray." Father Kevin kneeled in his boat and closed his eyes and prayed. The whole town prayed with him. Ma and Dad, Ken and me. Stephanie was there, too, praying for the fishermen and for their families.

"Amen," Father Kevin said.

"Amen," we all said.

That was the end of the blessing. Some folks hung around The Pier. Dad and Ma left for home. I think Ma was crying just a little. I wanted to join them and talk about things, or maybe not talk about anything at all. But for some reason I knew it would be better if I left them alone for a while. Besides, Ken was with me.

Mihn suddenly appeared – without Mai. "What a wonderful service!"

"I need to ask you about something," Ken said, and I thought for sure he was going to ask Mihn about that kiss.

"What's that?" Mihn asked.

But I guess Ken chickened out. "Do Buddhists have this kind of ceremony?"

"How would I know?" Mihn said. "I am a Methodist." Then he changed the subject. "Are you two ready?"

Ken didn't ask about the kiss. "Ready as I'll ever be."

"Me, too," I said. School started tomorrow, and we had something to do before Spring Break officially ended.

*"It was a final mission, a perilous but necessary journey into the heart of truth!"*

As we left the Pier, I turned and saw Father Kevin, still kneeling in his row boat and praying. And I saw Moby Dick, himself, out past the shallow bay, white and scarred and weary. As he breached, and then plunged back into the water, I remembered what Father Kevin had said about life and color and the choices we make, and all of a sudden, I knew why Moby Dick was white. I also knew that I had to live a more courageous life.

It started to rain.

# Chapter Twenty-Six

It continued to rain as we drove up the Summit. And I continued to think about courage, and about trying to live life in real time.

Even with a smashed-in grill that made the car look like it was wearing a hungry, metal smile, Ken's T-Bird still ran well enough to take us up past Otis' Electric Kitchen, to the mobile home park where Ronny Behr lived

This trip was Mihn's idea, of course. "Something good will come of this," he said. "I know it will. I promise it will."

"How do you figure?" Ken asked. "This could be a total disaster."

Zomb, sitting on my left shoulder, chimed in with either a snarl or a sneeze. It was hard to tell which, sometimes.

But Mihn was confident. "Ronny will appreciate the fact that we took time to come and see him."

"Then again," I said, "he might throw another orange at me." A thought suddenly entered my mind. "What happened to the orange that Ronny threw at me?"

"Beats me," Ken said. "I was too busy punching Ronny in the nose and getting myself suspended."

"I took it," Mihn said.

"You took the orange that hit your buddy in the

186

face?" Ken was stunned. "How come?"

"I took it home and then I gave it to Mai. She loves oranges."

"Wasn't it mushy on one side?" I asked.

"Not really."

"Did you tell her that I got smacked in the face with that orange?"

"Oh, yes," Mihn said. "I told her."

"And she didn't care?"

"Not at all. Like I said, Mai loves oranges."

And then, there it was. Oso Grande Trailer Park, just off the river. Lots of older, sagging trailers, a few new ones. Double wides. Single wides. Pickup trucks and propane tanks. Rusty lawn furniture. One of the trailers, a white double wide, had a handmade, woodshop project sign on the door with the words BEHR FAMILY burned into it.

"This must be the place," I said.

There were deer and elk antlers hanging along one side of the trailer and a white, older model pickup truck parked on the other. A wooden porch had been added and the grass around the building was neatly mowed.

Ken parked the T-Bird. "Last chance to reconsider."

"This will be a piece of ass cake," Mihn said. "You will see."

But I wasn't so sure.

Ken removed his goggles, told Zombie to stay put. The three of us got out of the car, and the rain slacked a tad.

"Here goes nothin," I started up the front steps, not knowing what to expect. There was a rocking chair on the porch. A bear, chainsaw carved out of wood.

Mihn joined me at the door. Ken took his usual position behind us. I took a breath, remembered what Father Kevin had said about courage, and knocked.

We waited. We listened. All we could hear was the rain in the trees and out on the river.

"It's nice out here," Ken whispered.

"Peaceful," Mihn said.

*"Did this quiet, forested setting conceal some form of riverbilly evil?"*

And then Ronny's grandfather opened the door. He was smiling.

"Mister Behr?" Mihn asked.

"Yes." Mister Behr seemed confused, but his voice was friendly. "Can I help you boys?"

"We would like to say hello to Ronny," Mihn said. "If you do not mind, of course."

"Oh." Mister Behr looked surprised. "Please come in." He backed out of the doorway.

The three of us entered the trailer. It was small, but comfortable and clean. No gun racks on the wall or car parts on the floor.

"Ronny's in the living room," Mister Behr said. We followed him. As we passed the small kitchen, I saw a young girl sitting at the counter and coloring. I assumed the girl was Ronny's sister. She watched us without any kind of expression.

Mister Behr waved us into the living room. "Some friends here to see you, Ronny."

Ronny lie on a hideaway bed on the other side of the room. There were pill bottles on a card table along with a glass vase with Scotch broom flowers in it. One get well card. Just one. Even hurt and bandaged, Ronny still looked mean. I guess I'd assumed he would look weaker, maybe spanked in a way.

**188**

Chastised. But no. Ronny looked as if he could still throw a mean punch – or an orange.

Mister Behr stood behind us. "Ronny?"

Ronny didn't answer or say anything. I couldn't tell if he was angry or embarrassed or just shocked to see the three of us.

"Hi, Ronny," I said.

Ronny sat up, inhaled through his nose and puffed up his chest a little. "What are you guys doing here?" He spoke with a slight lisp – from biting his tongue the other day, I assumed.

"Hello, Ronny," Mihn said.

"We just wanted to stop by and see how you were doing." Ken spoke in a friendly voice. "That's all."

"That's all," Mihn said.

"Did you bring me flowers?" Ronny asked. "Did you bring me some candy?"

"Easy, Ronny," Mister Behr said.

I heard Ken sigh, as if trying to say, this wasn't a good idea, and I thought maybe we should just wish Ronny the best and then get back down the mountain.

"We just wanted to see if there is anything we can do for you," I said. "That's all."

"That's all," Mihn said.

Ronny glared at me – just like when the paramedics brought him out of Don's.

We could hear the muffled sounds of rain and river.

Then I guess Ken thought the best way to end things would be with a laugh.

Ken: "A man is sitting in a movie theater when a whale sits next to him."

"Aren't you a whale? asks the man."

"Yes, I am, answers the whale."

"What are you doing at the movies?"

189

"I liked the book."

Nobody laughed. Not even out of politeness.

"I want you dumb shits off my mountain," Ronny said.

"Time to go," I said. "See you, Ronny."

"Is there anything we can get for you?" Mihn asked.

Ronny didn't answer.

Mister Behr walked us to the front door. On our way, we passed the kitchen again. Ronny's sister waved to us and smiled and I noticed the refrigerator and the dishwasher were avocado-colored.

As we stepped out onto the front porch, Mister Behr stopped us. "I've done my best to raise him right, but he's just like his daddy." Then he shook our hands, thanked us, and went back inside.

We headed back to the car. "Piece of ass cake, huh?" I asked.

Mihn didn't say anything.

"Well, we tried," Ken said. Then he stopped in his tracks and started yelling at Mihn: "What's the deal?" he asked, and there was real anger in his voice. "Don't lie to us!"

"What ass are you talking about?" Mihn asked.

"You can't deny it!" Ken said. "We saw you! We saw you kiss your sister! Right on the face!"

Mihn looked at Ken and then back to me, and I think he was about to make up an explanation, but then he took a breath, and told us the truth. "Mai isn't my sister. She is my fiancé."

A logging truck roared past the trailer park, coming off the Summit and headed toward Seaport.

"Our parents arranged it before we were born," Mihn said, "but we are in love."

190

"Is that kind of thing even legal?" I asked.

"I am sorry I lied to you guys," Mihn said, "but I knew you would think it was strange. We will get married when we are eighteen."

"Well, ain't that a kick in the head," Ken said. And I'm sure at that moment, his big heart was breaking.

"I am sorry, Ken." Mihn opened the car door and held the seat for me.

"It's OK." Ken got in the Bird, snapped on his goggles. He seemed more embarrassed than angry. "I'm a big boy."

"Oh, no," I said. Zombie was curled up in the back seat. He wasn't moving, and I had never seen him like that. "Zombie?" I reached over and touched him. Zombie was stiff. Zombie was dead. "Ken!"

Mihn looked back over his shoulder. "What's wrong?"

When Ken turned to see poor, dead Zombie, his head dropped to his chest. "Zombie," he said. "You dumb, pop-eyed rat."

What lousy timing. First, Ken finds out that Mihn is going to marry Mai, and then, he finds his pet ferret dead in the back seat of his Thunderbird. I didn't know what to do or say to make my friend feel better. I sure didn't want to see Ken cry. I had never seen him even come close to crying.

"What happened?" Mihn asked.

It wasn't deadly hot inside the car, or anything. Zombie's leash wasn't wrapped around his neck. There was no blood. "I think he just . . . died," I said.

"Zombie had a good run. Two good runs, actually." Ken got out of the Bird and took off his letterman jacket. He opened the back passenger door, lay his jacket on the back seat next to Zombie, and spread it out. Then he gently placed the poor dead ferret onto the jacket and folded it over. "The old boy deserves a rest."

I teared-up a little. Poor Zomb. He never bit or scratched anybody. And I wanted to believe that his attempt to mate with Mister Fishback's ear had come out of some loving place in his little ferret heart.

Ken looked around. "This is as good a place for a ferret to die as any."

"It's a beautiful place," Mihn said.

Then we left Oso Grande Trailer Park and headed back down the Summit.

About halfway to Seaport, we stopped at an old camper that someone had hollowed-out so that kids could use it as a school bus stop. Ken got out of the T-Bird. I didn't know what was going on and I'll bet Mihn didn't either, but we followed Ken and didn't ask any questions as he lifted one end of that camper and moved it several feet to one side. Then we watched as Ken opened the trunk, took out one of those short Army shovels, and started digging a hole.

Now, I understood. So, as Ken dug the grave, I retrieved Zombie – wrapped in Ken's letterman jacket. When Ken was finished digging, I handed the bundle to Mihn, and he passed it to Ken, who slowly, lovingly lowered both the jacket and Zombie into the grave.

"Didn't you say that your jacket cost a hundred and fifty dollars?" Mihn asked.

"Zombie was a million-dollar ferret," Ken said. Then he laughed. "Sounds like a great movie: *Zombie, the Million Dollar Ferret*."

Ken carefully filled in the grave and patted it down. "Anyone want to say a few words?"

"That crazy ferret had more energy and more personality than most people I know," I said, and that was the truth. "I'll sure miss him."

"Amen," Mihn said. "Good bye, my furry friend."

We stood there for a moment. Nobody said anything. And then Ken began to sing "Nearer my God to Thee," in that wonderful tenor voice.

I didn't know all the words, and did the best I could. Mihn, on the other hand, jumped right in. It was probably the most bizarre send off a ferret had ever received, let alone a ferret that had already died once.

But if that was strange, what happened next was even stranger.

As Ken dragged that empty camper back into place, covering Zombie and protecting him from any predators that might dig him up, I saw a hand claw its way out of the tiny grave. It was a girl's hand. It was Stephanie's hand. She was alive!

I screamed her name and ran at Ken, yelling at him to stop, and I reached under the camper and lifted and pushed and then I fell to my knees and started clawing through the dirt with my fingers and calling for Steph and crying until I dug poor Zombie back up again.

That's when I caught myself and stopped. My hands were dirty and my knuckles were cut and bloody. I could hear sound of cars and trucks on the road, and then I remembered where I actually was, and why. Ken stood by the road – with his back turned to me because I guess he didn't want to see me like that. Mihn was watching me and smiling just a little, but it was a forced, frightened smile.

"I'm sorry." I spread the dirt back over Zombie's grave. "I'm very sorry."

"It's OK," Mihn said.

Ken didn't say anything, didn't turn around.

"You better take me home," I said. "I need to talk to someone."

"Father Kevin?" Mihn asked. "That would be a good idea."

"Nope," I said. "I need to talk to my sister."

# Chapter Twenty-Seven

## Sunday Night

Ken dropped me off in front of our house on Desdemona Street.

I went straight upstairs to Stephanie's room. I didn't even think about it first or plan what to do or say and I didn't even count to five this time or gun up my Steve-O-Scope. I just opened the door and went in.

Like I said, Ma had kept it the same since Steph died: Same Bay City Rollers poster. Same Wizard of Oz books. Same grandma quilt on the bed. I stood in the middle of the room and just took it all in, in no particular order – and as prepared as I could be for any kind of reaction or emotion. Fear. Sadness. Relief.

"Hey, Steph." I didn't see her or hear her voice, and that was OK. "I go back to school tomorrow, and you know what, I'm glad. This has been one heck of a Spring Break. I feel like I've aged a whole year."

No voices. No images. I didn't try to suppress anything or dwell on anything. I just experienced one moment and then the next. I wasn't sure if I'd leave in a minute or an hour or ever. Maybe this would be a healthy, healing experience. Maybe it would send me to the funny farm.

I walked over to Steph's night stand and picked up a framed photograph that I hadn't seen in a long time.

It was a picture of Stephanie and Dad, out in the shop. In the photo, Steph's face is streaked with black grease and she is carrying a wrench that was about half her size. I remembered her face and her expression, but I was surprised at how much younger Dad looked.

"I took that picture." I put the photo back exactly where it had been, picked up another one and then put it back, too. Then I noticed a ceramic Brontosaurus there on the night stand. It was about six inches long and glazed with green and blue. I had made that Brontosaurus in art class as a second or third-grader and had given it to Ma as a Mother's Day present. I hadn't seen it or even thought about that Brontosaurus in years. What was it doing here?

I sat down on Steph's bed and ran a hand over the quilt. It was a lot like my own quilt except mine had more blue and Steph's had more pink in it. I lay back and looked up at the ceiling and remembered what Father Kevin had said about life and love and faith.

"What do you think, Steph?"

She didn't answer, but I was sure that Steph would tell me that life could be sad, but that it could also be exciting and funny and even wonderful every so often, and that it was wrong to try to hide from life because you never knew when it might end and leave you wishing you had done more living and less wishing, dreaming – and imagining things. Ma was going to die one day. Dad, too. Me, too. There was no way to escape it. And there was no reason to even try to run away from it. It was so much more important to live your life every single day and love the people in your life as much as you can and tell them you love them before they go.

"Thanks, Steph," I said. "I'll come back again

196

sometime. Maybe today. Maybe not. But I'll be back soon."

There. It was done. I wanted to cry, and I mean go to town. I wanted to sob, to bawl, to throw myself on the ground and pound my hands and feet like a two-year-old. I even tried to make myself cry, just to get it all out of my system, once-and-for-all time. But I couldn't cry. I just couldn't. And that was OK. So I got up from the bed, looked around the room one more time, took a deep breath, and left.

Then I went to my own bedroom room and started in on my homework for Ms. Ellerath.

# -Part Four-

"Then all collapsed, and the great shroud of the sea rolled on as it rolled five thousand years ago."
**– *Moby Dick*, Herman Melville, 1851**

"Gee, Mister Huston, I've never been able to read the damn thing."
**– Writer Ray Bradbury, when asked by director John Huston to read *Moby Dick* and then write a screenplay, 1953.**

"Time keeps on slippin' slippin', slippin'
Into the future."
**– "Fly Like an Eagle," Steve Miller band, 1977**

"Oregon is an inspiration. Whether you come to it, or are born to it, you become entranced by our state's beauty, the opportunity she affords, and the independent spirit of her citizens."
**– Tom McCall, 1973**

# Chapter Twenty-Eight

## Monday

Of course, Mister Fishback's Monster was the big topic of discussion when we went back to school. When did you see it? Did you puke? Were you there when it blew up? What do you think it was – really? The Monster was the biggest thing that had ever happened to Seaport. Ever. Bigger than when the Japanese bombed us in '42. Bigger than the Columbus Day Storm of '62.

Funny, thing, though. For just a week, or so, a fanged, tentacled, fuzzy beast had brought us all together, just like a storm or a sneak attack or an assassination. Ken had been right about monsters giving us meaning. Maybe that was the lesson we had learned by the end of our monster movie.

*The people all cheered*
*when The Monster exploded.*
*But then we missed him.*

Ken got his car fixed – for free, as part of our "financial understanding" with Les Schwab – and he didn't get kicked off the wrestling team or the chess team. All good news. But for some odd reason, Ken started calling Mihn "Mister Mihn," as in, "How's that chili mac, Mister Mihn?"

Mihn hadn't been changed by the experience, but Ken and I looked at him in a different way, now. He was almost a married man, after all. Mai started joining us for lunch, and that got kinda weird, especially for Ken.

Ronny Behr never came back to school. He stayed home, and we heard the school sent a special tutor to his house every day. We talked about visiting him again, but we never did.

I turned in my *Moby Dick* homework on time. I still wonder if Herman Melville – wherever he is – gets a big kick out of knowing that thousands of English teachers and literature professors have taught entire courses dedicated to unravelling *Moby Dick*, and that hundreds of thousands of students have struggled to explain his book.

And I wonder if Mister Melville would appreciate what I had to say about his great white whale.

# Chapter Twenty-Nine

## My Homework Assignment

### Moby Dick vs. King Kong

*Moby Dick* is a classic American novel, written by Herman Melville. One of the main characters in the book is a sea captain named Ahab who has dedicated his life to killing the white whale that bit off his leg. I don't want to ruin the ending of the story for anyone, but let's just say that Captain Ahab isn't very successful.

*King Kong* is a classic American movie, directed by Merian C. Cooper and Ernest B. Shoedsack. Kong is a fifty-foot ape that falls in love with a woman named Ann Darrow. Kong is captured, and brought to New York. He escapes his chains, and then climbs to the top of the Empire State Building with Ann in his hairy hand. Things don't end well for Kong, either.

What is the connection between a white whale and a black gorilla? Critics, college professors, and some high school language arts teachers, all say that classic tales like *Moby Dick* and *King Kong* contain symbols and metaphors that show deeper meanings.

For example, I recently read an article by a movie expert who said that because Kong is black in color, he is a symbol for the African slaves that were captured and brought to our country in chains. Those slaves were beaten, humiliated, and severely punished or even killed if they dared to love a white woman.

Literature experts seem to think that Moby Dick's white color represents some deeper meaning. White, they say, could represent purity, or innocence, or even God. Nobody I know can agree, however, and since Mister Melville is dead, we can't ask him.

After a week of thinking and asking other people about symbolism, I have come to the conclusion that Moby Dick's white color could be a symbol for life itself. White is not a color, after all. White is not good or bad, positive or negative. White is blank, and waiting for us to give it color and meaning in the same way that our lives are waiting for us to give them meaning. We choose. We decide. Hopefully, our choices and decisions will be positive.

Captain Ahab chose to color his life with selfish revenge. Ahab could not accept the terrible, painful things that life had done to him. He abandoned faith, and chose a life of hate, revenge, and terrible selfishness. Ahab could have retired from whaling, forgotten all about Moby Dick, and maybe even opened up his own chain of seafood restaurants. He could have lived to be a happy, old man, but he chose not to do that.

My sister, Stephanie, died a few years ago. I miss her every day, and wish I could bring her back. But I can't bring her back. I need to accept that fact, move on with my life, and be as positive as I can be. That is how Steph would want me to color my life. And it is the right thing to do.

Maybe I have figured out the great mystery of *Moby Dick*, but then again, maybe not. I think it is important to remember that before Merian Cooper died a few years ago, he agreed that *King Kong* as a symbol for slavery was an interesting interpretation, but very, very wrong. *King Kong*, he said, is just a simple adventure story, and nothing more.

Could it be that Mister Melville made his whale white in order to challenge his readers to ask questions, explore different ideas, and debate each other? *Moby Dick* might be just like one of those ink tests that psychologists use, and everybody that reads it can come to their own unique conclusion. Maybe that's why this book is considered a great literary classic.

I will conclude with a haiku:

*Moby Dick was white.*
*What does the whale represent?*
*Is there one answer?*

# Chapter Thirty

## After School

I stuck my head in the door. "Can I talk to you, ask a few questions?"

"Sure." Mister Fishback sat at his desk – hunched over and working, I assumed, on one very cool scientific project or another. It was good to see him out of handcuffs – thanks to Don, who just happened to have some handcuff keys in his back room.

I took my usual seat. "Thanks." And then I noticed that both of Mister Fishback's hands were dripping blood, and his white dress shirt was streaked with red. "Are you OK?"

Mister F. held up a jagged piece of black obsidian – volcanic glass – with two bleeding fingers. "I've been chipping away at this thing, trying to make the same kind of arrow point used by the Kalapooya Indians a hundred years ago, but I keep slashing myself."

"Maybe you should wear gloves, or something."

"Might be a good idea. Do me a favor, Steve, and get me some paper towels." Mister Fishback looked down at his stained shirt. "On second thought, ya *bettah* bring a whole roll."

I went over to the eye washing station, grabbed a roll of paper towels, and brought it over to Mister F's desk. "Here ya go." Then I watched as Mister Fishback started wrapping his bleeding fingers, one at a time. "I need to ask you about that thing down on the Ono Beach. What was it?"

"That OSU report was only partly accurate," Mister F. said. "I think those biologists missed something important, something really significant. Did you see that huge gash in one section of the thing?"

"I got a good close shot of it," I said. "Pretty nasty."

"That gash was more than just an injury," Mister Fishback said. "And it wasn't caused by a boat propeller. That was a bite wound. Wide, deep, and fresh. There were smaller gashes, too, and I think they might have been made by claws of some type."

Bite wound? Claws? Then I remembered those bizarre images and sounds that had lightning-flashed through my head when I touched The Monster on that first day. Wicked jaws and eyes coming at me from deep underwater. That awful, agonized howl. "What could've done that kind of damage?"

Mister Fishback shrugged. "I can't even imagine. But the animal that made those wounds is still out there. I'd hate to run into it in a dark alley, or out in Roddy Bay."

"Me, neither."

"I hope whatever it is lives way out, and way, way deep."

"Me, too."

We sat there for a while – Mister Fishback's blood slowly clotting, and me trying to imagine the terrifying animal that was, even now, cruising beneath the inky depths of the Pacific and hunting for its next unsuspecting meal. Whatever that mysterious beast was, and wherever it came from, one thing seemed certain.

*"That voracious, deep-sea nightmare was the real Mister Fishback's Monster!"*

Mister Fishback wiggled his mummy fingers.

"What are you going to do with the film you shot?"

"I'm going to shoot some extra stuff," I said. "Then I'm going to cut it all together like a trailer, and hopefully use it to get into film school."

"Trailer? Like one of the coming attractions you see before the movie starts?"

"Right," I said. "How'd you like to be in it?"

"In your movie trailer?" Mister Fishback seemed reluctant.

"I've got most of it story boarded in my head," I said. "All you'll have to do is just stand there on the beach for about fifteen seconds, and maybe shake your head sadly."

Mister Fishback thought for a second. "Can I wear my dead shoulder parrot?"

I didn't want to squash my actor's creative energy. "We'll shoot it with and without the parrot. How's that?"

"Deal."

# Chapter Thirty-One

## Friday, June 9, 1978- the Last Day of the School Year

I pulled down the movie screen at the front of Mister Fishback's classroom, held it, made sure it would stay there. How many washed-out, poorly-spliced, stuttering, sputtering, and impossibly outdated educational films had I watched on that old, glass-beaded screen? Then I turned to my fifth period audience. Stoners. Jocks. Sons and daughters of fishermen and loggers. All paying attention. To me. And I was ready. I felt brave, and it felt good to feel brave, and I thought that maybe I should've rented a tux for this occasion.

"You know how whenever you go see a movie," I asked, "and you always have to sit through a lot of coming attractions?"

A few nods and murmured yeahs and uh, huhs.

"Those coming attractions are called trailers, and I decided to take the film I shot at Ono beach during Spring Break and then make a trailer out of it."

A few confused looks. Nobody seemed to mind, though.

"So here it is," I said, "a trailer for a movie that doesn't exist. Lights, please."

Mihn hit the lights, and the room went dark.

"Thank you." I walked to the center of the room,

took a deep breath, and turned on both the movie projector and the cassette tape player at the same time. Then I pulled up a chair and watched my flick – along with the rest of my marine biology class:

# Chapter Thirty- Two
## The Trailer

Zombie sticks his head through a circular hole in a piece of cardboard. Around the hole are the words OVERHAUL PRODUCTIONS. But instead of roaring like the MGM lion, Zombie just stares with those mismatched eyes.

Low, ominous guitar music: "Frankenstein" by the Edgar Winters Group, played backwards, and with a finger on the edge of the record to slow it down a little. Green-blue waves curl and crash on the rocky, Oregon shore. A single arthritic pine tree clings to a rocky cliff, looking like a life-size bonsai. Storm clouds gather.

Ken, speaking in that Orson the Tiger voice: "We should have known."

Polluted water dumps into the Columbia River. A smokestack vomits ugly yellow smoke into the sky. Dead crabs float in the lapping surf. And then, there he is: Mister Ron Fishback himself, standing on the beach and watching out over the churning sea. He shakes his head sadly.

Ken: "This man of science, this humble biology teacher, found the creature, discovered it. Some even named the behemoth after him. They called it . . ."

Music blares as large block letters fill the screen as

Ken bellows the title: "MISTER FISHBACK'S MONSTER!"

More backwards "Frankenstein." My Brachiosaurus stands on some ancient shore, slowly chewing vegetation. A tribe of juvenile Tyrannosaurs hunt at the edge of an evergreen forest.

"Mighty beasts ruled the world before the dawn of man. These ferocious brutes were part of nature's grand balance."

Now, Mister Trammell stares out from the screen, and his white hair snaps and dances in the ocean wind.

"Native tribes knew how to live in harmony with nature and her children."

Tom McCall, surrounded by other dignitaries, stands at a lectern, smiling and speaking to the crowd.

"Modern men of wisdom and science warned us."

Ken, in close up, bites into a Hangtown Special. Then he smiles with his mouth half-open and half-full of chewed food.

"But we chose lives of hollow, selfish, indulgence. The inevitable result: a beast so horrifying, so disgusting, so completely nasty that we cannot show it to you in its entirety."

Flash cuts: Dagger-like teeth. A flipper with bones exposed. A curled tentacle. That awful, staring eye.

"Watch, as an entire city is repulsed, completely grossed-out! Nobody can cast their eyes upon the hideous deep sea fiend without becoming violently ill!"

People on Ono Beach, both common folks and VIPs – including Tom McCall – wretch, gag, and vomit.

"No one is safe!"

Les Schwab, multimillionaire, tire magnate, media personality, a rugged man of the land who built his

212

grooved rubber empire out of hard work, fairness, and honesty, a man powerful enough to send a goon to choke me out and steal this very film, blows chunks into his cowboy hat.

Mister Trammel, covered with filth and slime, emerges from inside The Monster. A helicopter, hovers above the sea. Army vehicles stand by.

"Our only hope – innocent beauty."

That soft focus, slow-mo shot of Julie Smith from the first day on the beach.

"But would beauty be enough?"

The big closer: "Thus Spoke Zarathustra" plays on the soundtrack, as Mister Fishback's Monster swells, and then erupts in repulsive slow motion. Internal organs spew from inside the thing and escape, uncoiling and tumbling, into the sky.

"MISTER FISHBACK'S MONSTER!"

Bones and body parts come raining back down. Bloody victims, running for cover. Broken windshields and bent fenders. A smashed car hood.

"MISTER FISHBACK'S MONSTER! See it, before it sees you!"

That bloody BEACH ACCESS sign.

Block letters: COMING SOON TO A THEATER NEAR YOU!

Mihn's voice this time: "Sponsored in part by Les Schwab Tires."

# Chapter Thirty-Three

And then it was over. My great premier had ended. I waited for the audience reaction.

To my surprise, people actually applauded. People I didn't even know, people who had laughed when I got hit in the face with that orange, clapped and cheered. The lights came back on.

"Great job!" Mister Fishback clapped along with everyone else. "Fantastic!"

"Thanks," I said.

One of the most popular girls in school – I can't even remember her name, now – reached over and touched Julie's shoulder. "You looked so pretty in the movie." I don't know if that popular girl was being sincere, or if she was just acting out of pity, or what.

"Thank you," Julie said.

"She is pretty," I said. I don't know if anybody laughed or hooted or said anything, because I just didn't care what anybody else thought

Julie looked at me, beaming, and looking prettier than I'd ever seen her.

"I was there," one of the jocks said. "That was pretty bush-league the way those Army guys took you down, Mister F."

"I guess Steve missed the part where I roughed up those MP's singlehanded," Mister Fishback said.

Everybody laughed, and I gave the spotlight, back

214

to Mister Fishback. I was done, and I was OK. I didn't need attention. I didn't want attention. I just wanted to make movies.

As I rewound my flick, something caught my eye, something outside the window of Mister Fishback's classroom.

It was that black Ultra Rex again, the one from that Friday before the break. And Pam Grier, dressed in gladiator armor this time, was back in the saddle, strong legs on either side of the Rex's neck and steering it back into the trees.

*"Her mission finished, at least for now, the mahogany-skinned beauty was on her way to another place and....hey, wait for me!"*

A thin, awkward man with slicked back hair and large eyeglasses came running across the football field and toward the tree line. Pam yelled at Movie Trailer Guy to hurry up. Then she held out a hand and pulled him up into the saddle with her. It was time for me to let Pam and Movie Trailer Guy go. I wanted to wave goodbye, but I didn't.

As the Tyrannosaurus Rex and his passengers headed back for the forest, a girl came running after them. It was Stephanie, happy and leaping and whole, just like she was before she was killed.

I didn't want to let Stephanie go. I needed her here with me – if only in memories. I guess Pam agreed with me. She backed up the Rex and turned it around, just like John Wayne used to do with a horse. It was a cool move. Pam spoke to Steph, smiling with those perfect teeth and letting her nostrils flare just a little. I don't know what Pam said to my twin sister, but Stephanie stopped, and she waved as the Tyrannosaurus strode back into the woods and disappeared.

I saw Julie Smith, looking out the window, too. I got a chill. Could she see what I was seeing?

Nah.

Could she? And then, for just a second I pictured her with a badass 'fro – which looked pretty odd.

# Chapter Thirty-Four
## That Night

Action! Ma's face filled the viewfinder. You could even see that tiny scar on her upper lip from that time she went over the guard rail in Lake Oswego. Then she got smaller. Then she got bigger again.

Zoom-in, zoom-out. We were in Ma's avocado kitchen, just the three of us: Ma, me – and my brand new, Minolta XL440 super eight camera, complete with zoom lens and microphone – another part of our deal with Mister Schwab.

"The school called today," Ma said. "I talked to a man named Erickson. He's the school counselor."

Cut! School was over. Was I in some kind of trouble? "What did he say?"

"He thinks maybe you should see someone. A specialist. A psychiatrist, maybe."

"Psychiatrist? Why? I'm not crazy."

"Are you happy? Do you like school?"

"Nobody likes school, Ma."

"Do you daydream a lot? Do you imagine things that aren't there? Do you hear voices?"

Now I knew what was going on. As far as Mister Erickson was concerned, anybody that fantasized about monsters and dinosaurs must be psycho – especially if those mental movies were narrated by Movie Trailer Guy. I wanted to laugh, especially now, since I hadn't threaded up Steve-O-Scope in a long time, but I knew Ma wasn't kidding around. "I have an imagination. Big deal."

She leaned in. "You have monsters on the brain, son. You should be thinking about girls and cars and sports. Do you have a girl friend?"

I knew if I told Ma about Pam Grier, I'd be in a straitjacket within the hour. And I wasn't sure about Julie. So I gave a vague – and I think, a fairly clever, answer. "Not yet."

"Mister Erickson thinks you might be autistic."

"Artistic?"

"Autistic. I'm not sure what it is. Neither does Mister Erickson."

I thought about all my Steve-O-Scope daydreams, and about the terrifying things I had seen and felt when I touched The Monster. Was I autistic? Were autistic people on some sort of special wave length?

I fully expected Ma to say something like, "No boy of mine is going to go around seeing and hearing things that aren't there. You'd better drop this strangeness, and I mean right now. I want you to shut down your little make believe movie studio, go get a commercial fishing license, and take a course in hunter safety by the end of next week!" But she surprised me. She didn't say any of those things.

She just said, "I just want you to be happy."

"I have good friends that like me, Ma. And I like them. We're all a little weird, but it's OK. We're all weird together."

Ma looked satisfied. For now. "I'll tell Erickson that we talked, that yes, you are odd, but not likely to jump out a window or murder anybody."

I told you Ma had a soft side.

"Thanks," I said.

"Promise me, here and now, that you'll tell me or Dad if things get out of control. OK?"

"I promise."

"I mean it!"

"I promise, Ma."

"I've lost one child in this lifetime," Ma said. "I will not lose you, too. I just won't, that's all there is to it." Ma didn't show any emotion at all when she said that. Then she went out to Dad's shop, pulled some elk steaks out of the freezer, and brought them inside.

Ken graduated that night. His grandmother was sick and his dad was up in Alaska, fishing, so the only people who applauded when the superintendent called Ken's name were me and Mihn – and Ma and Dad. Ma felt bad for Ken, so she went a little overboard, and fired off a long blast from one of those canned air horns that you weren't supposed to bring, but nobody had the guts to kick Ma out.

I saw the entire graduation ceremony without any Steve-O-Scopic fanfares or huge fireworks. But it was easy to imagine Ken being knighted for all of his bravery and loyalty after receiving his diploma.

After the ceremony, we took Ken to Don's Last Stand since that was his favorite place on Earth. He ordered his usual Hang town special, and we all managed to look somewhere else during the few minutes it too for him to eat the thing.

I hadn't been back to Don's since that awful day when Ronny was hurt, and I really didn't want to go back, but I knew it was important to deal with that bad memory before it turned into a complex.

We all ate and laughed and had a great time. We were all happy for Ken, and I think he knew he was part of a family.

# Chapter Thirty-Five

## Saturday Night - Live

Dave the weatherman does a pretty fair impression of Boris Karloff: "And now, here's the host of *Creature Feature*, Professor Ravenswort."

The professor appears. For the last time. "Good evening, monster fans, and welcome to this very last installment of *Creature Feature*. You heard correctly. This will be our last show. A program on another network, a program that is broadcast live from New York, has taken away most of our viewers. I have seen this so-called comedy show, and I must admit that I don't get it. Aliens with cone-shaped heads. Chubby guys wearing killer bee costumes . . ." The professor shakes his head sadly.

"Tonight, we will present an underrated classic from the year 1955, and a fitting farewell: *It Came from Beneath the Sea*, starring Kenneth Tobey, Faith Domergue, and a giant octopus, animated by none other than Mister Ray Harryhausen.

Watch closely folks. The huge cephalopod makes its first appearance on the Oregon Coast, squashing a hapless policeman, and leaving huge sucker tracks in the sand.

This movie might remind some of you of an incident that occurred in Seaport a few months ago, when a strange sea beast washed-up after a storm. I went to Seaport to see the dead creature. It was not a pleasant experience, but I made a friend, a young man who impressed me with his love of monsters and movies. I didn't ask his name, and he didn't ask mine, but I hope he is watching tonight."

The camera moves in for a close up. The professor smiles. "This movie goes out to you, sir. Good luck in Hollywood."

Fade to black. The last movie begins.

# Epilogue

I was finally able to sit down with our granddaughter to watch *King Kong* on my new Blu-Ray machine. Amy is six, which, as far as I'm concerned, is the perfect age to see that classic movie for the first time.

She didn't like it, though. First, she started griping about the movie being in black and white, and asked if there was a colorized version on the Internet. Then I guess she got bored during the first half hour or so and started texting one of her friends. During the scene where the natives of Skull Island kidnap Fay Wray, Amy asked, "Is this movie racist?" And even though I was fully prepared to console Amy with a trip to her favorite place in the world, Baskin Robbins, she wasn't the least bit fazed when Kong, bleeding and defeated, finally let go and took the long fall down to the street. But what really hurt me the most and made me wonder if we were doomed as a civilization, was what Amy told her dad, my son, Kevin, when he came to pick her up.

"What did you think of the movie?" Kevin asked.

"That big monkey looked fake," Amy said.

*King Kong took the fall.*
*It was beauty killed the beast.*
*Fay Wray was worth it.*

## Fin

# About the Author

When Steve Sabatka was five years old, he saw the original, classic King Kong for the first time. He hasn't been the same since. As a kid, Steve started making 8mm movies, animating clay dinosaurs in miniature jungles, and dreaming of becoming the next Ray Harryhausen. But by the time Steve was a senior in high school, stop motion had become a dying art. Steve started writing – and dreaming of being the next Ray Bradbury.

When he was in college, Steve met Fay Wray in person at a film festival in Dallas, Texas. So effusive was his praise and appreciation for Ms. Wray, that the aging actress felt it prudent to alert theater security guards. Happily, no charges were preferred. Steve also met his childhood idol, Ray Harryhausen - and actually shook the hand that gave frame-by-frame life to Mighty Joe Young, and Gwangi.

Steve lives in Newport, Oregon, just a few blocks from the ocean, and teaches at Newport High School – home of the Cubs. *Mister Fishback's Monster* is his first published book.

Wherewolf by Franchisca Weatherman.  978-0-9833773-7-5

When a pack of werewolves hits a small southern town, the local Sheriff realizes this is one case he can not solve alone. He calls in the F.B.I. to help him take down the killers that are taking the lives of the local teens. When the wolves abandon the town for the streets of New Orleans during Mardi-Gras celebrations, the hunters become the hunted in an all-out war where no one may survive....

## Morningstars by Nick Kisella

While at his dying wife's bedside, Detective Louis Darque is offered a chance to save her by his biological father, the demon B'lial, but at what price?

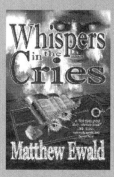

## Whispers in the Cries
### by Matthew Ewald
### 978-0-9833773-6-8

Hunted by the shadowed entity of his grandfather's past and its brethren of demonic beasts, Randy Conroy must survive the nightmare his grandfather could not. A thrilling ghost tale of the Queen Mary and haunted souls.

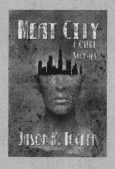

## Meat City & Other Stories by Jason M. Tucker    978-0-9842136-9-6

Take a trip along the arterial highway, and make a left at the last exit to enter Meat City, where all manner of nasty things are clamoring to greet you. Granger knows what it's like to kill a man. When the corpse of Granger's latest victim staggers to his feet though, all bets are off. These and other slices of horror await you on the raw and bloodied streets. Enjoy your visit . . . .

## Nevermore by Nik Kerry

. When Raven's world comes crashing down around her and her thoughts turn to suicide, this is exactly what she does. As she swings the last swing of her life, she jumps off, sprouts wings, and flies away to another world where she finds a group of teenagers just her age who accept her into their lives.

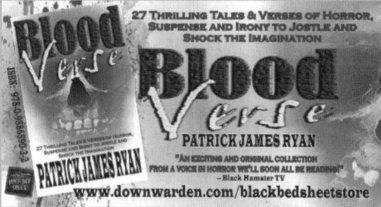

We employ and recommend:

## Foreign Translations

# Cinta García de la Rosa
(Spanish Translation)
Writer, Editor, Proofreader, Translator
cintagarciadelarosa@gmail.com
http://www.cintagarciadelarosa.com
http://cintascorner.com

# Bianca Johnson
(Italian Translation)
Writer, Editor, Proofreader, Translator
**http://facebook.com/bianca.cicciarelli**

# EDITOR STAFF

## Felicia Aman
http://www.abttoday.com
http://facebook.com/felicia.aman

## Kelly J. Koch
http://dressingyourbook.com

## Tyson Mauermann
http://speculativebookreview.blogspot.com

## Kareema S. Griest
http://facebook.com/kareema.griest

## Mary Genevieve Fortier
https://www.facebook.com/MaryGenevieveFortierWriter
http://www.stayingscared.com/Nighty%20Nightmare.html

## Shawna Platt
www.angelshadowauthor.webs.com/

## Adrienne Dellwo
http://facebook.com/adriennedellwo
http://chronicfatigue.about.com/

Made in the USA
Charleston, SC
21 February 2017